VERDICTS
& VIXENS

BOOKS BY KELLY REY

Jamie Winters Mysteries:
Motion for Murder
Mistletoe & Misdemeanors (holiday short story)
Death of a Diva
Motion for Misfits (short story in the Killer Beach Reads collection)
The Sassy Suspect
Verdicts & Vixens
A Playboy in Peril

Marty Hudson Mysteries:
Sherlock Holmes and the Case of the Brash Blonde

VERDICTS & VIXENS

a Jamie Winters mystery

Kelly Rey

VERDICTS
& VIXENS

CHAPTER ONE

———

Except for the lawyers and the clients, the law firm of Parker, Dennis was a pleasant enough place to work. Lots of rich wood and old books and pricey furniture. It was warm in the winter and cool in the summer, and it had indoor plumbing and a stocked kitchen.

My name is Jamie Winters, and I liked to delude myself that my job as executive assistant was just a blip in my professional trajectory. But after a year and a half, I knew better. I was in my thirties, hadn't gone to college, and wasn't particularly ambitious. My trajectory was pretty much the same as the Hindenburg's.

I was in the kitchen eviscerating a Twinkie on a Thursday morning in mid-June when the temperature chilled, and I looked up to find Janice Iannacone, the firm bookkeeper, sitting across the table staring at me.

A word about Janice. That word is *terrifying*. When she wasn't trampling the support staff, she manipulated Parker, Dennis's finances like Play-Doh. I had reason to believe she also embezzled, and that reason sat in the parking lot and cost $50,000.

"Hello, Jamie," she said.

That should have been my first warning.

"I need a favor," she said. "You know Oxnard Thorpe is one of Howard's best clients."

Lawyer-speak for *richest*.

"He's marrying Sybil Sullivan a week from Saturday," she said. "Howard needs someone from the firm to be there. He asked me. I'm asking you."

I stared at her. "What?"

"It's no big deal," she said. "It's just a wedding. I thought you might like to help me out."

I couldn't imagine why she would think that. We weren't exactly besties. It was hard to warm up to someone who opened each workday with the phrase, *"Get out of my way."*

"I don't think so," I said.

"I can slip an extra hour of pay into your check," she said. "Howard wouldn't notice."

"I don't think so," I said again.

"A hundred bucks." Her voice was grim. "How long does it take you to earn a hundred bucks?"

She ought to know. She was the one who cracked open the piggybank to pay me.

But I knew bargaining power when I heard it. "A thousand," I said.

She snorted. "Get real. I'll give you five hundred."

I considered it. I'd be getting paid to go to the wedding of a person I knew nothing about by a person I knew too much about.

Then again, I was constitutionally incapable of doing the Macarena.

Then again, she was offering me someone else's money.

Then again, that someone else was Howard Dennis. And Ken Parker, the Sleeping Beauty of the legal world. But mostly Howard Dennis.

Was I so mercenary that I'd trade my long-held principles for a few dollars in the bank?

What a stupid question.

"Five hundred," I said. "Cash. In small bills."

She raised an eyebrow at me.

"And I'm not doing the chicken dance," I said.

An hour later, I was at my desk trying to wrestle Howard's indecipherable handwriting into a formal complaint when the phone rang.

"You'll never believe this." It was Maizy Emerson, my landlord Curt's niece. Maizy was an uber socially conscious seventeen-year-old genius with blue hair and a talent for situational improvisation.

"That doofus driving examiner failed me," she said.

"Again."

Maizy had failed her first test because she'd initiated a high-speed chase in the middle of it. Which hadn't stopped her from driving any more than *Cop Rock* had stopped people from watching TV. She got her cars from a shyster named Honest Aaron who didn't require a driver's license, rented by the hour, and offered discounts if the cars had bloodstains and missing seats. Because she refused to drive her parents' gas-guzzling SUV on eco-principle, she insisted on taking the test in my car. Which was fine, except I drove the Methuselah of cars, and it had broken down on the way to the DMV on her last test date. Maizy was a lot of things, but patient wasn't one of them.

I hit Save and sat back. "I'm sure there's a story here."

"There's an injustice here," she said. "And it's not my fault. I rented a '71 Pinto from Honest Aaron for the test. He should've told me not to make right turns."

I closed my eyes. "What happened?"

"The passenger door fell off," she said. "Don't worry, the examiner landed in the grass. After he rolled across the street. You might think that's a bad thing, but road rash clears up pretty quick."

Actually, I was thinking I shouldn't get in a car with Maizy ever again.

"He was lucky," she said. "He didn't see that little electrical system fire. I'm starting to think a '71 Pinto isn't a very safe car."

"So he failed you because you made him fall out of the car," I said.

She snorted. "I didn't *make* him fall out. Is it my fault he didn't use the bungee cord? But that's not even the important part."

The examiner would probably disagree.

"The DMV blacklisted me for *three months*," she said. "Can you believe that? It's not like I couldn't finish the test. It just took a little more concentration. We didn't even hit anything."

That was something less than a Clarence Darrow-esque defense.

"It's cool, though," Maizy added. "Honest Aaron felt

bad, so he discounted a boss 240Z. It's got a bike rack and everything. You'll see it later. I'm coming over to Uncle Curt's for dinner. I'll park around the block so he'll think I rode my bike over."

"I don't want to lie to Curt," I told her. Curt and I had a thing going. I couldn't exactly define *thing*—it changed a lot, depending on whether I was a murder suspect or he was shirtless.

"It's not a lie," she said. "He doesn't need to know how *far* I rode it. It's all about results with me."

It was all about insanity with her. Still, it was probably better for her to get Honest Aaron out of her system before she became an adult in the eyes of the criminal justice system.

The future Mrs. Thorpe, Sybil Sullivan, showed up a couple hours later. She was less than a stunning beauty. Her sharp, pointed features and raised eyebrows gave her the look of a perpetually surprised ferret. Her outfit seemed expensive, but linen only took you so far. The last time I'd seen someone like her, it had been in a movie, when a house had fallen on her.

"Get Howard," she said, but less politely. "Oxnard Thorpe has an appointment to discuss revisions to his will." She pivoted to reveal the Oxnard Thorpe previously hidden behind her 100-pound heft. His skin hung on him, and his skull was pink and shiny between patches of wispy white hair. His red-rimmed but sharp eyes were taking liberties with me that I didn't like.

He offered me a gnarled tree stump of a hand. "You must be Julie."

"Jamie," I said, at the same time Sybil said, "Oxie, not yet."

Not yet? He didn't look like he had much time to wait.

I tried to free my hand. The old geezer was stronger than I'd expected. After he petted and stroked and squeezed it to his satisfaction, he gave it back to me.

Sybil's gaze was as penetrating as an x-ray. "Is Mr. Dennis here or not?"

Oxnard threw out his elbow to poke his dearly beloved with it and got her right in the oversized designer bag. She never felt a thing. The bag came away with a puncture wound.

"Dear, why don't you stay down here and talk to June for a bit."

Oh, no. He wasn't pawning Miss Personality off on me.

"That won't be necessary," I said. "I have a lot of work here and—"

"She'd love to talk to you," Oxnard informed us. "You two can get acquainted while I consult with Howard." He did another full body scan on me. I was starting to feel like I was at the airport. "If you would tell him I'm here, dear."

After a fawning Howard had scrambled downstairs to whisk Oxnard off at a brisk shuffle, Sybil folded herself into the empty secretarial chair across the room.

I focused on the monitor, where my cursor blinked insistently: *Therefore...* Maybe I should charm her with small talk since she was the fiancée of Howard's pet client. Problem was, I couldn't think of a thing to say. Except:

"So you're getting married," I said.

Oprah had made it look so easy.

"Oxie pursued me for months before I agreed to go out with him," she said.

I couldn't imagine why.

"I was lucky to meet the man of my dreams," she added.

She was marrying the Crypt Keeper, and she called that lucky?

"By the way, I should thank you," she said. "Janice told me you're my maid of honor."

I looked up. "*What?*"

"My maid of honor quit yesterday. She said I insulted her just because I told her to lose thirty pounds and color all that gray hair."

Why would she find that insulting?

"I don't have a lot of female friends," she said. "For some reason, no one else wanted the job. So Howard asked that lovely girl of his, Janice, but she's scheduled to donate bone marrow and then drive senior citizens to doctors' appointments all day. She said you volunteered to step in."

How had I let Janice scam me out of half of a weekend? Oh. Right. Because she'd neglected to mention *maid of honor* when she'd been bribing me to take her place.

Speaking of bribes, Sybil was busy spending mine.

"You'll have to buy a better bag." She wrinkled her nose

at my $20 Walmart purse.

I loved that purse. Why spend $300 for a designer handbag to carry around $30?

"In fact," she said, "you'll have to get a better haircut, too. And for God's sake, pluck those eyebrows. And whiten your teeth. And it wouldn't hurt to—what's the matter with you?"

"I'm fine." My lower lip was trembling, but I was pretty sure it was just cold from the air conditioning.

She rolled her eyes. "Do you have to be so difficult about this?"

I was being difficult? She was lucky I wasn't impaling her on one of Oxie's elbows.

She huffed out a sigh. "Fine. You need some stroking. Janice said you were capable. Feel better now?"

Capable. Wow.

"Well, if you don't want to help me out..." She started blinking her fake eyelashes, trying to conjure up a tear. It was like watching spiders take flight. "Here," she said. "In case you change your mind."

An invitation landed in front of me. Lots of cream and peach with a little satin bow in the corner. I could appreciate a good card stock. Especially since Maizy had taught me how to get through any locked door with it.

I pushed it away. "I can't be your maid of honor. I don't even know you."

She pushed it back. "You know enough."

"Really," I said, "I wouldn't be comfortable. It wouldn't be right."

"You don't have to be comfortable," she said. "You just have to be there."

This was starting to sound like my sex life.

"The ceremony is at nine," she said.

"In the *morning*?"

She rolled her eyes. "At night, of course. I wanted a romantic midnight ceremony, but Oxie's schedule couldn't accommodate anything that late."

Probably conflicted with his bedtime.

"I want you there," she said. "You're hired."

Last time I'd heard those words, it had led to this job. I

wasn't going through *that* again. Even if Janice was embezzling five hundred bucks for the occasion.

Although I *could* put that extra money to good use. Sure, there was that whole saving for retirement thing, but I made next to nothing, drove a decrepit Escort, mooched meals off my landlord, and shopped the Walmart clearance racks. I didn't see a lot of golden years ahead of me.

"I already have a job," I said.

"Nice to see you have a sense of humor," she said. "I'll expect you next Friday at one for rehearsal."

Howard's voice grated through the intercom. "Does Jamie Winters still work here?"

"She'll be there," Oxnard's disembodied voice said.

Sybil stepped aside and there he was, shriveled up behind her again. I don't know how they did that. Those two should take their act to Vegas.

"Howard would like to see you," he told her. "I'll wait here with Julie."

"Mr. Thorpe—" I started, but I didn't know what else to say. Except… "My name is Jamie. And I should get back to work."

"Oh, keep an old man company," Oxnard said. "I won't let them fire you."

He had a way of leering that made me want to slap off his liver spots.

"Would you happen to have anything to drink, Julie?" he asked.

I ran down the beverage list. "And my name is Jamie," I added.

He wanted coffee, so I poured him a cup. He wanted milk, so I added milk. He wanted two sugars, so I added two sugars. Then he wanted tea, so I poured it down the drain and started all over again.

"So," I said, just to keep the mood light while I fumed, "how did you two meet?"

"The usual way," he said. Whatever that meant.

I did the sugar and milk thing, this time with a teabag. While I was sliding it in front of him, he snaked his arm out and pinched my backside. Which made me jerk and splash most of the tea into his lap, which probably didn't contain working parts anymore. His mouth flew open. No sound came out, but his teeth did, dropping with a splash into the remains of his Lemon Zinger.

Howard picked that moment to barge into the kitchen. "Jamie, did I or did I not tell you that I needed you to—" He froze, his gaze bouncing from Oxnard's hands on his privates to his grimace to my expression of guilt. "You're fired," he told me.

"I didn't do anything," I said. "Mr. Thorpe—" I hesitated, "—startled me," I finished. "It was an accident."

"I should say it was." Howard handed Oxnard some paper towels. "Sir, I'm very sorry. Do you need medical attention? I can't imagine how this happened. And—" He held up a hand when I started to tell him. "—I don't care to know. It won't happen again. Today is her last day."

Oxnard fished his teeth out of his tea, stuck them back in his mouth, and said, "Nonsense. I expect to see her when I come back. I find her charming."

"You do?" Howard frowned at me, clearly not seeing it.

I stood there and stared, charmingly.

"She was quite right," Oxnard said. "I startled her. Completely my fault. Although maybe I'll ask for iced coffee next time, hm?" He chuckled, which got Howard chuckling in the way that sycophantic suck-ups tend to do.

Next time I'd dump the whole teapot on him.

CHAPTER TWO

———

For the rest of the afternoon, I did the usual secretarial things for the usual lack of appreciation, and when the clock hit five, I headed for home.

Home was on the second floor of Curt Emerson's house in Maple Grove, on a street full of trees and responsible, lawn-mowing nine-to-fivers. Curt was as good as it got when it came to landlords: rent was on a sliding scale, food was guaranteed, studliness was a side benefit. He had a business degree but worked as a package delivery driver because he didn't want to spend his days in a cubicle wearing a tie. In his spare time, he kept his house clean, his lawn landscaped, and his barbecue grill in good working order.

I found Maizy with him in the backyard when I got there. Maizy's ten-speed was propped against the house. She slouched in her chair wearing skinny jeans, a midriff shirt, and Doc Martens, her hair poofed and Carolina blue. Heavy on the black eyeliner. She'd painted her nails white with a little ruby set into each of the two middle fingers to aid in nonverbal communication.

Curt had swapped his uniform for faded jeans, running shoes, and a royal blue T-shirt that did magical things for his shoulders and chest. He had dark brown hair, darker brown eyes, and a perpetual five o'clock shadow that totally worked for him.

Over in the corner of the patio stood Vern, the silver Stud of Death mannequin who Maizy had acquired through dubious means to help us solve our last case. Vern was pretty hot for a guy with no face, all rounded muscles and hard planes. Usually he hung out in the basement, holding the rack for Curt's pool table. Guess Vern had needed some air.

To be honest, Vern freaked me out a little.

Curt smiled up at me over the top of the grill. "How's life at the asylum?"

"Same old," I said. "Janice bribed me to go to a client's wedding in her place. And volunteered me as the maid of honor. Good news, the bride hired me."

He frowned. "Why's she hiring bridesmaids?"

I did a palms-up shrug. "Don't ask me."

"I think that's practical," Maizy said. "Avoid the bouquet brawl and the sappy speeches."

"Some people like the sappy speeches," Curt told her.

"Some people like calamari, too." She turned to me. "Who's the groom?"

I cracked open a can of Coke. "Have you guys ever heard of Oxnard Thorpe?"

"Sure," Maizy said. "The Adult Diaper King of New Jersey."

I blinked. "The adult…what?"

"He founded No Flows," Curt said. "Adult diapers? *Live life in the dry lane*?"

"Incontinence is a major problem," Maizy said. "I hear that one out of every, like, five people over thirty has an incontinence problem. Is that true, Uncle Curt?"

Curt grinned. "Nice try, Maize."

"Dry or not," I said, "he almost got me fired after I spilled a cup of hot tea on his tidbits."

Curt smiled, showing me the full force of his dimples. It was stunning. "Tell me you did that on purpose."

"I did it when he pinched my butt," I said.

Maizy sat up straight. "That's sexual harassment. You could sue him. Is there a bruise? Let me see."

I frowned at her. "I'm not showing you my butt."

"Why not?" she asked. "I'll let you see mine."

"I'll let you see mine," Curt said.

"You can see Vern's," Maizy added.

I glanced at Vern. He might have leered at me. It was hard to tell since he had no face.

"I don't want to see your butts," I told them.

"You're so provincial," Maizy said. "*God*."

It wasn't a matter of provincial. It was a matter of the safety pin holding the elastic waistband of my underwear together.

Curt stacked the burgers onto a plate. "So are you going to do it?"

"Howard wants someone from the firm there," I said.

"Then Howard should go," he said.

"I'll do it," Maizy said. "But not for five hundred. I won't get out of bed for less than eight."

"You get out of bed for Alpha-Bits," Curt told her.

"That's different," she said. "Marriage is a trap. Why hook up with some loser who'll just spend your money?" She put the burgers on the table. "By the way, can I borrow twenty bucks?"

Curt and I looked at her.

She shrugged. "My earning power is in its infancy."

We sat down.

"I think you should go," Maizy told me. "I'll come with you if you want. You get in tight with Oxnard Thorpe—you've got it made. Hey, maybe he'll give me a loan. I could use some cash."

"Need a new belly button ring?" Curt asked her.

"I'm thinking of making the move from CZ to real diamond," she said.

"Nice," he said. "Maybe you should buy some whole shirts while you're at it."

She rolled her eyes. "You always say that, Uncle Curt."

"It's my job," he said. "And you always ignore me."

"That's *my* job," she said. "What do you think, Jamie?"

I shuddered. "There's no way I'm getting near that pervert again."

"You know the rent is due," Curt told me.

"Once the wedding is over," I said. I waited a beat. "It might be nice if you came with me."

"I already told you I'd go," Maizy said.

"Not you," I said. I glanced at Curt. "You."

"I appreciate the thought," he said. "But I told Cam I'd help him frame out his addition."

"Oh, yeah," Maizy said. "I heard my parents talking about that. My mom said the only way he'd get a man cave is if he built it himself. Why do all guys want man caves?"

"To get away from teenagers," Curt said.

"Good one," Maizy told him.

"What's more important?" I asked. "Framing a man cave or making me happy?"

He waggled his eyebrows at me. "I can think of a better way to do that."

I felt that waggle down to my toes. And other places.

"Don't worry about him," Maizy said. "I've got your back."

She could have it. I was saving the good parts for Curt.

CHAPTER THREE

———

There had been a few changes at the firm since one of its founding partners, Doug Heath, had made his final summation. Mainly that another founding partner, Howard Dennis, had rechristened the firm Parker, Dennis, because he wanted it to sound less like a personal injury mill and more like a big city firm that handled multinational class action suits. I was tired of fielding calls asking for Mr. Parker Dennis and I'm sure the directory information people stuck pins in a Howard doll on a nightly basis, but my opinion mattered about as much as a sale mattered to a kleptomaniac.

Then there was Wally Randall, Boy Lawyer. Wally was tall enough to be naturally imposing, serious enough to speak to an examined life, and pompous enough that he had already commissioned his judicial portrait. He'd been in practice for two years.

Another one of Howard's ideas had been office meetings, although nothing went on at Parker, Dennis that didn't filter through the support staff first. So at two fifty-five Monday afternoon, I took my seat in the conference room next to Missy Clark. Missy was a fellow drudge in name only, one of those rare people who had life figured out. Easy when you had a pretty face, a knockout body, and all the goods on your boss.

The paralegal, Donna Warren, was already there, since she spent most of her time in the conference room fondling law books and hiding from clients. Donna occasionally showed hints of a spine, but invariably her true character crept back to peek out from behind a corner.

Janice slipped in at the stroke of three and stood in the corner across the room without looking at me. Smart.

Howard swept in on a current of grim impatience. Howard's grimness was his sole discriminating feature. The concept of Casual Fridays was foreign to him, as was civility and a good haircut. He believed that no phone call should last longer than three minutes, that his ascension to the Bench was inevitable, and that civil juries were inherently pro-defense. Howard was not a happy man, but he was a busy one. He was usually leashed to a briefcase, a trial bag, or an expandable file, and labored under this burden much the same way Jacob Marley had labored under his.

The senior partner, Ken Parker, strolled in behind him, sat down near the head of the table, nodded and smiled at us, yawned, and closed his eyes. Ken was the perfect example of what a dignified gentleman lawyer should be, even if he'd passed his prime five years ago.

Wally hustled in on Ken's heels, trying to squeeze around him to get the seat closest to his idol, Howard. He didn't make it and had to settle for being two seats removed.

Following all of them was a cleaning woman of mid-something age. Her salt-and-pepper hair was cut short. Her pantsuit was mud-colored, paired with a matching plastic headband and Earth Shoes.

"Quiet, people." Typical Howard, always with the pleasantries. "Meet Eunice Kublinski. Eunice recently passed the bar and has agreed to bring her legal talent to Parker, Dennis."

So Howard had found a rookie to take Doug's place. Not that her lack of experience mattered—it was probably a benefit. For the next year or two, Howard and Wally would dump grunt work in her lap, saving the glory of fat settlements and bloated jury verdicts for themselves.

"A few facts," he forged on. "Eunice attended—" He looked at Eunice.

Eunice looked back at him.

"—college," he prompted.

"University of Coventry." She swallowed visibly. "Online."

Howard paled. "Coventry. And for law school—" Back to Eunice.

"Harvard," she said, practically whispering.

"Harvard?" Wally repeated in disbelief.

Eunice nodded. "Harvard Academy of Law and Mortuary Sciences."

Silence.

"So." Howard clapped briskly. "Let's welcome her to the firm, shall we?"

I'm not sure how welcome she felt after a tepid round of applause and a snort from Wally.

Howard was trying to coax up a smile with no lips. "Why don't you say a few words, Eunice?"

"I'm very happy to be here," Eunice said obligingly, but she didn't look very happy. More like petrified. Even Donna was peeking over the top of her book with sympathy. "I'll sue lots of people," she added.

Howard beamed approvingly. "We look forward to that. Thank you, Eunice." He waved her off, and she collapsed into a chair, blotting her forehead. He scowled at the rest of us. "I'm sure you'll each do your best to make Eunice feel comfortable as she settles in."

There was some noncommittal murmuring.

"After all," he said, pushing his luck, "we're a family here."

Giggles floated over the top of Donna's book.

"Now get back to work," Howard snapped. "Or you'll all be out on the street."

If it was a family, it was a dysfunctional one.

CHAPTER FOUR

———

The rest of the week was a maelstrom of boredom, fatigue, and aggravation capped off by the realization that Mick Jagger was right: you can't always get what you want. I'd wanted Oxnard Thorpe's house to fall off the map before Friday, but it was just where Sybil had said it would be, in a ritzy gated enclave. Lots of grand columns and floor-to-ceiling windows and French doors plunked down on a lush lawn fringed with rampant flowers. The knockoff statue of Michelangelo's David in the circular driveway tinkled gently in the fountain. David could have used some No Flows.

Shaking my head, I squeezed in behind half a Mercedes dealership. My Escort sat there like the pimple on a teenager's nose on prom night, leaking blood spatters of oil and polluting the atmosphere even with the engine off.

Oxnard answered the door. "Julie." He groped for my hand.

I was determined not to give it to him. "Jamie."

"Of course," he said. "Sybil's in the sitting room with Lizette. She's waiting for you."

I stepped into the foyer and was immediately goosed by Oxnard. Yelping, I leaped to my left, straight into a three-legged occasional table. The vase on the table teetered back and forth before somersaulting to the floor. Miraculously, it didn't break. Until the table crashed to the ground on top of it, and then it shattered into hundreds of slivers.

Sybil materialized in front of me. "What was that racket?" She noticed the ex-vase, and her face practically melted.

"I, uh…" I swallowed. "He, uh…"

Oxnard managed to play innocent while I felt as guilty as John Dillinger at a bankers' convention.

"I certainly hope you aren't this clumsy at my wedding," she snapped. "Look at this mess!"

I looked, not at the mess, but into the sitting room, where a motley lineup stood. Lots of leg and cleavage and bleached and teased hair. They were watching me like I'd just kicked Oxnard's cane out from under him. Figured they hadn't turned when he'd been using my backside as an ambulation device.

"Don't fret," Oxnard said. It wasn't consolation as much as command. "The vase is fully insured."

"You did this on purpose," she hissed at me.

More like the groom had done it on purpose.

"It was an accident," I said.

Sybil fondled a piece of vase. "My engagement gift," she moaned.

He gave pottery as an engagement gift? What a romantic.

"Maybe you can glue it," I suggested. "That Gorilla Glue is pretty good stuff."

"One doesn't glue a $750,000 vase," Oxnard snapped.

That vase—I glanced at its earthly remains—was worth three quarters of a million dollars?

"Come, my pet." Oxnard squared her shoulders, dusted her off, everything short of a pat on the backside. He'd already gotten that out of the way, with me. "Don't ignore your guests. I'll tend to this." He tended to it by snapping his fingers and barking orders at the underling that scurried in to clean up the mess.

Sybil dragged me into the sitting room where the lineup had melted away. "Jamie Winters, meet my wedding planner, Lizette Larue."

Lizette Larue juggled a laptop in one arm and pumped my hand with the other. The one wearing six hundred bangles. Our handshake sounded like a symphony of wind chimes. "You make quite an entrance," she told me with no trace of a smile.

"Those ballet lessons are finally paying off," I said.

She studied me for a few seconds before turning to Sybil. "Friend of the family?"

Sybil sighed. "The new maid of honor."

"I fear for this wedding," Lizette said and flounced off. I'd never seen anyone flounce before, so I watched until she disappeared. It was very dramatic.

"Help yourself to some hors d'oeuvres." Sybil waved at a sea of empty surfaces. "There may be something left in the kitchen."

As long as that something wasn't her. Between the bride and groom, my skin was ready to crawl off.

The kitchen was a study in austerity. Black granite, stainless steel, white cabinetry. No sign of food there, either, except for that tray half hidden behind a gorgeous brunette talking on her cell phone.

"They're not paying me enough to put up with that old geezer," she was saying. "Do you know he grabbed my—"

I cleared my throat. The brunette gave a start and dropped her phone in the tray of…was that shrimp? Darn. I never liked shrimp.

"You startled me." She fished her phone out with two fingers. "I didn't know anyone else was here."

"I didn't hear anything," I assured her. "So you're being paid, too?"

She poured some Perrier onto a napkin and wiped down the phone. "Who'd do this for free?"

Was the entire bridal party on the payroll? I felt cheap.

"That guy's got his hands everywhere," she said. "Good thing I'm getting a commercial spot out of this."

"You're an actress?"

"If you say so." A few more wipes, and the phone disappeared into a tiny clutch. "I'm Dusty Rose. Kudos for breaking that hideous vase. Wish I'd have thought of it."

"It was an accident," I said. "He grabbed my—"

"Yeah, he grabbed mine, too." She shrugged. "Doesn't matter how old they are, men are all alike."

I nodded again. Like I had a clue about men.

"It's the Viagra," she said. "Too bad it doesn't give them any more finesse."

I thought of Curt and said nothing. If Curt had any more finesse, I'd need a defibrillator.

"Well." Dusty gave me a high wattage smile. "Time to earn my big break. I've been waiting *forever* for this. No more pimple cream layouts for me." She glided away.

Not sure that she'd moved up in the world.

"She's a piece of work, isn't she?" a voice asked behind the hanging rack of pots and pans.

I turned to see a Helen Mirren knockoff clutching a champagne flute, looking after Dusty. The way she was swaying back and forth, I doubted she could actually see her. On the other hand, *I* could see that behind the impeccable hair and makeup, she was about two decades older than the rest of the bridal party.

"And to think I took off work for this," she added. "What was I thinking?"

Evidently she'd been thinking there'd be free booze.

I shrugged. "I thought she seemed nice."

"Nice." She wrinkled her nose. "The woman models *diapers*, for God's sake. You're not one of them, are you? You don't seem the type."

That explained the similarity among the women.

"I'm Bitsy Dolman." She slapped a business card into my palm. *Dolman Personal Shopping* with a swanky address in a nearby town. Interesting. When I looked at Bitsy Dolman, I didn't see swank. "Give me a call sometime," she said. "I'm semi-retired, but you could use a professional's help. How long have you known the bride?"

"I don't," I said. "Mr. Thorpe is a client, and I'm here on behalf—"

"At least she had the sense to hire Lizette," Bitsy plowed on. "At my recommendation, naturally."

"No offense," I said, "but it doesn't seem like you really want to be in the bridal party."

She let out a cackle. "Bridal party! Don't get me started on *that*."

No problem there. I backed away. "See you at the wedding."

"Wedding." She snorted. "Don't get me started on the wedding. And the groom. Don't get me started on *him*."

I left Bitsy to her ranting and rejoined Sybil and Lizette. I might not have found food, but I had found an idea. Maybe there was an easier way to earn Janice's bribe.

"Are you sure I'm the best choice for maid of honor?" I asked Sybil. "Bitsy Dolman seems much more…"

"Sophisticated?" she said.

"Refined?" Lizette suggested.

I frowned. "Experienced," I said. "I've never been a maid of honor. I really don't know what I'm doing."

"You'll be fine," she said. "As long as you don't break anything else."

"That's the thing," I said. "I can't guarantee that. I'm pretty clumsy."

"It's probably the shoes," Lizette said, giving my flats a disdainful glance.

Hey, I never pretended to be *Vogue* material.

"It might be my inner ear problem," I said. "It makes me dizzy, and I tend to fall a lot."

"I haven't seen you fall," Sybil said.

"But how much have you seen me stand?" I said. "I sit a lot. My leg muscles are very weak. They can barely hold me up some days."

"I haven't noticed you had weak legs," Sybil said.

"It's because of my foot problem," I said. "My foot problem makes it painful to walk."

"Sounds like we should have paramedics on standby," she said. Very deliberately, she plucked a tissue from the box on the table, dabbed at her eyes, and said, "I can't believe you want to abandon me the day before my wedding. Oxie wanted me to ask Abigail to be my maid of honor, but I said no, I want Jamie."

"You should've asked Abigail," Lizette said. "She has fewer medical problems."

"Who's Abigail?" I asked.

"It doesn't matter now," Sybil said. "I asked *you,* you said yes, and now you're saying—"

Geez. "Forget it," I cut in. "I'll get a few Ace bandages."

"Make sure they match your dress," Sybil said.

CHAPTER FIVE

———

At five o'clock on Saturday night, I tore myself away from a *Saved by the Bell* rerun featuring Mario Lopez's dimples to head for the shower. My cat, Ashley, remained curled up in a tight little ball on the sofa, snoring gently. I envied her. The most pressing things on Ashley's weekend schedule were naps and gynecological self-exams.

I did the best I could with my hair and face, then hauled my bridesmaid's dress out of the box. Turned out its pretty peach-colored face had fooled me. On its hanger, the dress had been chic and sophisticated. On my body, it was Vegas Strip, and not in a touristy way.

At seven, I gracefully stomped to Oxnard's door in my comfortable stiletto heels. A plump fifty-something woman in a maid's uniform answered my ring. Her nametag read *Pandora.*

"The solarium." Pandora pointed the way before plodding off, head hanging, the very picture of nuptial jubilation.

The solarium was all windows and greenery and soaring arrangements of white roses on either side of a makeshift altar. Rows of padded chairs lined an aisle defined by even more white roses. I stood in the doorway, admiring it.

"It's about time you showed up."

Sybil appeared beside me in a satin robe and high heeled slippers, the kind worn by divas on soap operas. She glanced out at the back nine that was Oxnard's yard. Hundreds of tea candles floated on the in-ground pool, and thousands of tiny white lights sparkled in the trees and bushes. Yards and yards of white lace and silk were draped about with casual artistry to lend an air of class and to hide the trash cans. It would be gorgeous after dark, if the marriage lasted that long.

"Oh, for God's sake." She sliced across the room. "I told Lizette I wanted the shades *down*." She stabbed at a remote control and cream-colored shades descended until the solarium resembled a luxe jail cell with no view and a thug for a roomie.

She snapped, "Come," and clattered along at a breakneck pace down a hallway, up a set of stairs, and finally into a fabulous master bedroom suite. I wasn't dressed for wind sprints. I stood in the doorway panting like a gazelle on the Serengeti. I really had to add some cardio to my workouts. Right after I added some workout to my workouts.

She threw herself onto the duvet. "Oxie cheated on me."

I leaned over, hands on knees, to catch my breath. "What?"

"He cheated on me," she repeated.

"He *did?*" I sensed a reprieve. "Are you getting married today?"

"It's not like he can actually *do* it," she said. "He can hardly *see* it. But he gives it his best shot."

I had the pinch marks to prove it. "Are you still getting married today?"

"It's the *intention,"* she said. "He was fawning all over that Dusty Rose. What girl could resist him? Powerful men are an aphrodisiac."

So were oysters, but I wasn't going to date one of them, either.

"So are you getting married today?"

She hauled herself upright. "Well, soon I'll be Mrs. Oxnard Thorpe. I'll have more money than Dusty Rose could even dream about. He'll pay for embarrassing me like that. Just you wait."

Turns out I didn't have to wait long.

By the time Sybil had speared herself into her tasteful red sequined wedding dress, everyone had gathered in the solarium with lots of foot tapping and glancing at watches. Lizette Larue, wearing a light green sheath and a cashmere cardigan the color of Colombian emeralds, jingled about with a scowl as if she was sure someone was going to screw up something. I recognized the women from the luncheon playing the parts of friends of the bride.

There were his-and-her wizened faces with Oxnard's predatory eyes, and I figured them to be his brother and sister. Bitsy Dolman was there, slouched beside an elegant man with very white hair and a millionaire's tan. She was clearly half-toodled, but she could still follow the scent of money. Every now and then, she slid the man a sideways glance full of longing. He didn't seem to notice, probably because she wasn't strapped to his wrist on a platinum band.

And in the last seat of the last row, wearing a purple gown straight out of junior high prom night, her blue hair hidden under a hideous feathery saucer of a hat, her arms and legs crossed, her Doc Martens bouncing impatiently, sat Maizy.

At nine o'clock, Oxnard took his place, bland classical music filled the air, and Sybil made her entrance, her red dress standing out against the white decor like a puddle of blood. She barely glanced at her groom, not that he would have noticed. He was busy winking at Dusty Rose behind Sybil's back. I wondered why a moneybags like Oxnard Thorpe would let his bride storm down the aisle to some generic *Eternal Romance: Classic Love Songs* CD.

The officiant launched into some rambling opening remarks. After about ten minutes—during which I think I heard someone say, "Will you get on with it? *God!*"—he mumbled a few words that couldn't possibly have been heard beyond the front row before inviting us to applaud the happy couple. And we were foisted off on Pandora, who scurried about with a huge silver tray as if she was on a deadline. When she'd dispensed with the hors d'oeuvres, she disappeared into the house, practically dragging the tray behind her.

Maizy was nowhere in sight. That couldn't be good.

"Well, that's done." Sybil was beside me. I hadn't even heard her coming. Smoke made more noise than she did.

"Congratulations," I said. "Everything went off without a hitch."

"Except for the old windbag." She pointed her chin toward the officiant. He was chatting up the Oxnard look-alikes, who nodded and frowned and shook their heads in unison. It was fascinating to watch, like a parlor trick you couldn't quite grasp.

Sybil moved off to the head table, which was round rather than rectangular, so that she wasn't exactly next to her husband, but rather around the bend from him. If he ever showed up. He and Dusty had their heads together in deep discussion across the room.

"Jamie!" Sybil bellowed. "Don't spill anything on that dress or you won't be able to return it."

That drew some glances, and all of them seemed to be saying "what a cheapskate." I slunk over to her side and grabbed the first champagne I could get my hands on, wishing I had the nerve to throw it on her.

Lizette showed up a few seconds later. "Your husband sent me over for the check."

Sybil bobbed and weaved to keep an eye on him. "What check?"

"Balance due," Lizette said. "It's payable today according to our agreement."

"Oh, that." Sybil did a dismissive little hand flap. "You'll have to get that from him."

Lizette glanced at me. I arranged my expression carefully to read *Don't look at me, I'm not responsible for the money, and could you send over Pandora with some food?*

"He told me to get it from you," Lizette repeated patiently.

"Don't bother me with that now," Sybil snapped. "I'll put it in the mail."

Becoming the Adult Diaper Queen of New Jersey sure hadn't mellowed her any.

Lizette's lips tightened. "Fine." And she stormed off.

I felt terrible for her, being stiffed after planning this decidedly third-rate affair. And jealous, because she got to leave early.

"You know you have to pay her," I told Sybil.

"What for? *I* didn't hire her." She didn't even have the grace to be ashamed of her cheapness. "Get a load of the two of them," she groused, shooting daggers in Oxnard's direction.

"They're probably talking business," I said, just as Oxnard did his squeeze-and-claw routine with Dusty's hand. Dusty did not seem pleased. In fact, she'd flushed deep red. I looked at Sybil. Who was looking at Oxnard. Who was looking at Dusty.

Sybil drained her champagne and reached for Oxnard's. "I'm cutting her pay."

Five minutes into the reception, and I could see it wasn't going to end well. A few guests had already slipped away like inmates who'd suddenly discovered an unlocked gate. The rest were swilling martinis and eyeing the clock, impatient to move on to their next social obligation or maybe just out of this one.

Snippets of conversation floated over to me: "…like a hooker in that getup" and "…don't get me started on *him*" and "…believe she's returning that dress?"

"Congratulations, Mrs. Thorpe." The white-haired object of Bitsy Dolman's affection towered over the table.

Sybil didn't bother to react. "Herman."

He clamped a hand on her shoulder and bent to plant a smacker on top of her head. "You make a beautiful bride. Where's your new husband?"

She shrugged him off and pointed her flute in Oxnard's direction.

He patted her shoulder and let his hand fall. "Well, I'm sure you two will be very happy together."

"Oh, get off it, Herman," she snapped. "I'm his fourth wife. It's hardly true love."

What a romantic.

Herman glanced my way. "Call me if you need me," he said.

"I have a husband now," she said.

We all glanced over at Oxnard and Dusty.

"I'll just be on my way," Herman said. "Good luck with your marriage." He glanced at me again, this time with pity, and marched off.

Looked like as long as I sat near Sybil, I'd never be in a crowd.

"Who was that?" I asked.

"That," she said, "was Herman Kantz, the man who covets my husband's money."

I knew I'd had the right idea by hiding my emergency stash under Ashley's litter box. No one with a nose would ever check under there.

Sybil snatched the champagne glass out of my hand. I hardly noticed. I was watching Herman and Oxnard chatting while Dusty made herself scarce. But within a minute or two, the chat got heated, Herman got red, Oxnard got loud, and Dusty reappeared ostensibly to smooth the waters. Only Oxnard had no intention of being smoothed. Without warning, he threw his drink into Herman's face. Herman blotted his cheeks with a monogrammed hankie while Bitsy Dolman came streaking to his defense with a fistful of canapés that she launched at Oxnard. They pinged off his chest with cheesy little splats.

That was when Dusty pivoted on her five-inch heels, clutching a fistful of bacon-wrapped pigs in a blanket, and opened fire until Bitsy's perfectly shellacked hair was draped with bacon bits and the room smelled vaguely like a luau.

"Oh, no, she doesn't," Sybil snarled, grabbing a basket of breadsticks from the table. She heaved them at Dusty like javelins. One of them went wide, spearing Oxnard in the throat. He went white, clutched his neck with both hands, and stumbled backwards from the room.

Which prompted the Stepford Oxnards to avenge their brother. Except Oxnard's sister had chosen a plate of Caesar salad to make their stand. They plunked a crouton off Sybil's shoulder and sat down again, exhausted.

Pandora chose that moment to return from the kitchen with a full tray of food. She took one look around, and her arms dropped. The tray crashed to the floor, spilling perfectly good filet mignon everywhere.

Pandora turned and walked out.

Herman Kantz had disappeared after his champagne shower.

Bitsy skirted past Dusty and slipped into the house, presumably to hunt for Herman.

Dusty gave Sybil one last glare and followed Bitsy, presumably to hunt for Oxnard.

The Stepford Thorpes, sufficiently recovered from the exertion of tossing lettuce leaves, lowered their brows (in unison) and crept away arm in arm, in no hurry to hunt for anyone.

Sybil stormed after all of them, probably to chase them to their respective cars.

And just like that, the reception was over.

Not for me. I planned to sample that filet mignon that had landed in an arrangement of roses and those roasted potatoes that had rolled beneath a canopy of baby's breath. I left the green beans on the floor. I'd never been much for veggies.

Five minutes later, Maizy sat down beside me wearing jeans and a black long-sleeved T-shirt. "I never knew weddings were this much fun."

"Where have you been?" I asked between bites.

"Here and there," she said. "Mostly there." She pulled out her cell phone and snapped a picture of the room. "I thought these people were going to be a bunch of stiffs. Thanks for inviting me."

"I didn't invite you," I said. "And where did you get that hideous dress?"

"At a yard sale. Three bucks."

"You paid too much," I told her. I took a bite of potato. Perfection. Just to be sure, I shoveled the whole thing into my mouth.

"Why are you in such a bad mood?" Maizy asked. "You just made half a grand the easy way."

It hadn't felt easy to me. I'd rather have stayed home in bed with Mario Lopez's dimples.

"Don't wait for me," I said. "I'm sure you have Honest Aaron's Z outside."

She snorted. "Get real. I have more class than that."

Despite all sartorial evidence to the contrary.

"I rented a stretch limo," she said.

I almost choked on the potato. "Don't tell me you wasted your money on a limo."

"Of course not," she said. "I might have suggested they bill Oxnard. What's another three grand to a moneybags like him?"

I stared at her. "It cost three grand to get here?"

"It cost a hundred bucks to get here," she said. "It costs $2,900 to get to Niagara Falls. That's where my friend Lainey really wanted to go. I hear it's pretty there. You and Uncle Curt should check it out sometime."

A dull pain throbbed behind my eyes. "You told them to bill Oxnard for your friend's trip to Niagara Falls?"

"What, he can't spend $2,900 on his alleged great granddaughter?" She nodded toward the shaded glass wall. "What's out there?"

I pointed to the remote control lying in a puddle of green bean juice. Maizy shook it off and pointed it at the window. The shades obediently slid upwards, revealing the thousands of sparkling lights. "That's pretty," Maizy said.

Oxnard Thorpe was floating face down among the tea candles in the swimming pool.

Maizy and I looked at each other.

"But that's not," she said.

CHAPTER SIX

———

I stood at the edge of the pool, staring down at Oxnard while trying to take deep breaths despite the almost painful tightness in my chest. He hadn't moved so much as a finger; the only mobile part of him was the wispy hair streaming out from his head like tentacles from a squid.

Maizy rushed up with the long-handled pool skimmer and thrust it at me. "Here. See if he's really dead."

I took an inadvertent step back. "You do it."

"I don't want to poke him," she said. "It's disrespectful."

"Well, I don't want to poke him, either," I said.

"How about this. We'll float him closer to the edge and haul him out."

"Still disrespectful," I said. "Why don't you jump in and bring him closer?"

"I'm not going to jump in there," she said. "There's a dead guy in there. I don't touch dead people."

"Fine." I grabbed the skimmer. "I'll do it." I stretched it out, misjudged the distance, and thwacked Oxnard soundly on the back. No reaction from Oxnard. *My* reaction was immediate uncontrollable shaking that made my teeth clack together. I tried again and managed to hook him by the leg. We knelt on the concrete apron and pulled him to the edge. "Do you know how—" I began.

Maizy had already whipped out her ever-present latex gloves and pressed two fingers to Oxnard's neck. After a few seconds, she peeled them off and stuffed them in her pocket. "Poor old dude."

I looked away, but the image of Oxnard's shriveled, pasty, floating corpse was seared into my brain. "We need to call the police," I said. "And we need to find Sybil."

"Agreed," Maizy said. "But first give me your keys. We need to move your car."

"Why are you worried about my car right now?" I asked.

"I'm always worried about your car," Maizy said. "But if someone drives by, we don't want to be the last ones here. People will notice. Maybe they already have. It wouldn't be good for us."

Good was a relative thing. I took another peek at Oxnard. Still dead.

I stood up abruptly. "You're right. We should get out of here."

"Now you're talking," Maizy said. "I'll meet you upstairs. Give me your keys."

I frowned. "Why would we go upstairs?"

"Because we should find out who killed him," Maizy said. "And that's where the clues are."

There were so many things wrong with that. Starting with: "Why should *we* find out who killed him?"

"If not us," she said, "Who?"

"The police?" I suggested.

"I'm not saying they can't help," she said. "Don't worry—I'm going to call them. Now are you done hoovering your plate of cholesterol and starch? Because we should probably get moving before he starts stinking up the place."

Oh, gross.

"I was *not* hoovering," I said indignantly. "I was just hungry. And how do you know what's upstairs, anyway?"

Maizy rolled her eyes. "Where do you think I was all night?"

I was getting that feeling again. The one where I pretended to know what I was doing while Maizy galloped a mile ahead. "Don't tell me you were skulking around this house."

"It was a self-guided tour," she said. "And once you get past the walk-in closet full of boxes of No Flows diapers, it was pretty much like every other multi-million-dollar house."

Eww. Also, TMI.

"Come to think of it," she said, "my aunt Lulu at the assisted living has a closet full of diapers, too. She sells them to other residents at five bucks apiece. Aunt Lulu always did have an entrepreneurial spirit."

"Has it occurred to you that maybe no one killed him?" I asked. "Maybe it was a horrible drunken accident."

"I don't think so," Maizy said. "He was drinking apple juice and Metamucil."

I stared at her. "How do you know that?"

She shrugged. "Because I mixed it for him. How much of that stuff are you supposed to use, anyway? Is a half a cup good?"

I kept staring at her.

"Doesn't matter," she said. "Water and the bridge, right? I'll take care of the car. Then we'll get started."

I waited there, but only because I wasn't feeling too good. Finding dead bodies tended to up my general quease factor. Or maybe it was the farce of a wedding that had done that. I wasn't one of those women who'd dreamed of their wedding day since birth, but I liked to believe true love was a possibility, like six-pack abs and twelve-hour lipstick. Even though Oxnard Thorpe had been a handsy old geezer, he hadn't deserved to die on his wedding day. Alone.

Speaking of that, it was awfully strange—and convenient—that no guests had been around when Oxnard had met his maker. Also strange that I hadn't even heard a splash. Of course, I'd been busy not hoovering filet mignon to pay much attention.

I looked up through the solarium's glass roof. It was past eleven. The sky was cloudless, and the moon was full, lending a startling brightness to everything except my mood.

Maizy was back, pretty unconcerned for someone who was trespassing on a murder scene. "I just thought of something," she said. "Do you think he died during nicky-nack?" She waggled her arms and fingers around, indicating, I presumed, conjugal bliss.

"With who?" I asked. "The bride disappeared along with everyone else."

"Maybe he was a do-it-yourselfer," she said.

My nose wrinkled all on its own. "In the *pool*?"

"He seemed like a free spirit," she said. "You don't know. I mean, if you ignore that he was a couple hundred years old and probably tired easily, it's possible."

Had Sybil deliberately boinked Oxnard into a heart attack and then run off? I couldn't see it. I didn't *want* to see it. If Oxnard hadn't been drinking, my theory of a drunken tumble was dead in the water, pardon the expression.

"We'll call the police in a minute," she said. "Follow me."

I followed her into the pitch-black foyer. "Why are the lights off?"

"It's better that way," she said.

It was *never* better that way. I picked up the pace to catch up to her. "Shouldn't we make a statement or something?"

"About what?" she asked. "Do you know something I don't know?"

Unlikely under any circumstance.

There was something spooky about the house, with the cool darkness and the knowledge that Oxnard wasn't coming back somehow lending an air of abandonment. Hard to achieve that, with priceless antiques and paintings and hideous designer furnishings scattered about. Sans a particular vase, of course. It was too quiet, without so much as the white noise of the HVAC system.

Within a half dozen steps Maizy had blended into the shadows. She was no more than a disembodied face in the darkness when she turned. "You plan on standing there till morning or what?"

Definitely *or what*. I followed her down dark hallways, past closed doors, and up a tiny elevator—an elevator! —to the third floor, where we finally arrived at Oxnard's office. I knew we'd arrived when she stopped walking and I ran smack into her back. Well, it wasn't like I could see her or anything.

"You take the desk," she told me. "I'll check the master bedroom. Maybe there's a safe in there. Remember, no lights." And she disappeared into some dark crevice in the corner of the room. I heard a door open, and she was gone.

I groped my way across the floor, smacking my shin on something to the left and whacking my knee on something to the right, stopping when I hit the desk. With my hip. The desk, as it turned out, was the approximate size of the *Eisenhower*. It was made of some dark wood, burnished to a mirror gloss. It held a slew of papers and a single photo in a silver frame. I held the frame up to my nose for closer inspection. The Stepford Thorpes smiled gummy smiles back at me. I put them down, facing the other way, and picked up the papers, angling them toward the mostly lightless window to try to read them. Lying on top was Lizette's bill with a balance due of—I squinted harder—the national deficit. No wonder she'd wanted her money. She probably had her eye on a chateau in the Alps. I folded the page into quarters and stuffed it in my bag, deciding I'd try to smooth things over with Lizette. When I questioned her about an alibi.

I kept sifting through the papers, my curiosity piqued. Letterhead with the No Flows logo, a pint-sized David wearing an adult diaper. Classy. Purchase orders and invoices reflecting that there was big money in the circle of life. A few contracts, evidenced by all the *wherefores* and *hereunders*, between Oxnard as CEO of No Flows Incorporated and Allison Madeline Cartwright, Jalen Jefferson, and Caroline Kirby. Oxnard hadn't signed any of them. The others had. Allison had dotted her "I" with a little smiley face. Oddly, while the contracts were of recent date, everything else seemed to be a year old.

The top drawer was full of the usual: rubber bands, pencils, pens, paper clips, a stack of risqué Polaroids featuring a very talented dark-haired stud lounging casually on throw pillows in a black Speedo. He had such a come-hither expression that I couldn't resist carrying him over to the window for a better look to see if I recognized him from, say, Sunday services. His name, stamped on the back along with his significant measurements (funny, he seemed taller than 5'9") and professional credits ("man waiting for bus"), was Rod Rockstone. Allegedly.

For the sake of thoroughness, I flipped through the rest of the stack, stopping when I saw a familiar face. Dusty Rose, wearing a string bikini. Yowza. Compared to her, I was built like a garden stake. So this was the No Flows roster of diaper models that Bitsy had railed against. They were practically identical except gender and hair color. And I had to say, having given the matter intense consideration, Rod Rockstone had a leg up on his competition.

You never knew when something could come in handy, so I slipped his photo into my pocket and returned to the desk. Oxnard had been surprisingly organized. His files were alphabetized, his collection of DVDs numbered, and his telephone directory filled with nice large clear printing that enabled me to read Bitsy Dolman's address and number even in the dark.

Bitsy Dolman? It took a second to register. Maybe Bitsy had served on some charity board or other with Oxnard. She might be a pretty good fundraiser, and what else did she have to do with her days once she got her drinking out of the way?

Although I had her business card, it seemed like a good idea to jot down her home address, too. I found a piece of notepaper and scribbled down her information. It gave me another way to contact her, and I couldn't very well take the entire telephone directory. It was much too large to fit in my skinflint purse.

When I thought I'd found everything there was to find, I decided to find Maizy. I picked my way across the floor, into the hallway, past some hideous framed Rorschach tests, but I couldn't locate the nexus of my breadcrumb trail, the elevator. I could have sworn we'd left it just beyond the portrait of the Stepfords in their younger years, their 70s. I tried not to look at it as I scurried past in case their eyes followed me.

Finally, after groping my way down another hallway, I found the master suite. Maizy wasn't there. She wasn't in the en suite, either. Weak moonlight pushed through the glass block window behind a ginormous soaker tub, faintly illuminating a lifestyle I'd never have.

"Find anything?" Maizy asked from behind me.

I whipped my head around so fast I nearly broke a bone. "Will you stop sneaking up on me like that?"

"I'm not sneaking," she said. "I'm being prudently silent. So what'd you find?"

"I found Bitsy Dolman's home address and phone number."

"The drunk lady, right? Is that all?"

I patted the pocket where the photo of Mr. Right was safely tucked away. "That's it," I said.

"Maybe she was doing nicky-nack with Oxnard," Maizy said. "On the side. I hear money is an aphrodisiac."

I thought of Sybil whining about Oxnard's affair. Maybe that should have been affairs, plural.

We got on the elevator, which had somehow moved to a different hallway, and rode to the first floor. Everything was quiet. The lights were still off. Oxnard was still dead.

Ninety minutes later, after we'd given our statements to the police, we settled into the Escort. Maizy had parked by the side door, having stuffed the car with a box of No Flows along with brooms, mops and a vacuum cleaner in an effort to disguise us as the cleaning crew. Not sure where she'd been going with the No Flows, but I was pretty sure the cleaning supplies were a not-so-subtle suggestion that I planned to ignore completely.

"He was awfully old for nicky-nack, wasn't he?" Maizy asked once we were on the road. "I thought those parts just shriveled up after a while. Unless he had the little blue pill. Then he could probably nicky-nack all night."

"You mean the little purple pill," I said.

"I don't think so," she said. "I think it's the one with the possible side effect of *you could die*."

That didn't narrow the field much.

"Anyway," she said, "I didn't find anything in here, either. Some massage oil and a box of glow-in-the-dark condoms."

Eww.

"Why would you want it to glow in the dark?" I asked.

"Maybe he liked to pretend it was a light saber," she said.

Eww again.

"So," Maizy said, "Guess we need to talk to the new widow."

"Guess so," I said glumly. "But I'm not waiting for her here."

"Agreed," she said. "This place has lost its panache. We'll do it tomorrow."

Not if I could help it.

CHAPTER SEVEN

———

I couldn't help it.

Maizy tapped me on the shoulder at eight a.m., simultaneously waking me from a sound sleep and performing an unscheduled stress test. "Time to get started."

My eyes shot open while my pulse rocketed into the red zone. I could practically taste my heart. "What are you doing here, Maizy?"

"We agreed we'd talk to Sybil today." She scratched Ashley's ears. Ashley pushed her head into Maizy's hand and purred.

"It's not today yet." I pushed myself upright. "How did you get in here, anyway? I know I locked my door."

She snorted. "Single cylinder deadbolt. You want to call that locked, fine by me. Come on. Get ready. She has a nine o'clock appointment at Zara's."

An uber-chic spa that charged $200 for a massage. I could barely afford to drive past it.

I stuck my legs into jeans. "How do you know that?"

"I'm not just a pretty face," Maizy said. "I can also dial a phone."

I had to have clean socks somewhere. I got up to dig in the hamper. "You called Sybil Thorpe?"

"It's been done," she said. "There." She pointed to a pile of laundry in the corner.

I found socks and a hoodie sweatshirt with a zipper. "Think this is okay for Zara's?"

"Absolutely not," Maizy said.

Her outfit was jeans and a hoodie sweatshirt. "You're wearing the exact same thing," I said.

"But I'm wearing it with style," she said.

Whatever.

I did my best with very little equipment, and we headed downstairs to my car. Curt was already on his way back to his brother's house. The neighborhood was still half asleep. So was I, so I flipped Maizy the keys.

"Good news," she said. "Sybil agreed to let us do what we do. Well, actually she said 'It's late, I need to get some sleep.' But the gist was there."

"What do we do?" I asked.

"We're detectives," Maizy told me.

News to me.

"Ipso facto," she said, "we investigate. You can't be shy in this business."

"This isn't a business," I said. "This is…" I trailed off. What was this? Not a hobby, because hobbies were supposed to be enjoyable.

"Sure it is," Maizy said. "It's just a not-for-profit at the moment. That's all gonna change, because we rock."

I was pretty sure I didn't rock. On my best day, I was the driver of the getaway car while Maizy was the evil genius behind the operation.

I watched the world slip past the passenger window for a few minutes. It slipped by pretty fast. Maizy tended to regard speed limit signs as suggested minimums.

"Do you think it's possible that she killed Oxnard?" I asked after a while.

She shrugged. "What have our investigations taught us?"

"That I should have gone to college?"

Maizy sighed. "They've taught us that we don't rule out anyone."

Oh. That, too.

"Except," I said, "it makes no sense to hire us if she did it." Unless she had no fear of actually being found out. Which meant she had no belief in our abilities. That made two of us.

"It could be a psychological ploy," Maizy said. "She might think if she hired us, we'd never suspect her. Of course, hire implies pay. We're doing this for good will."

Then we were wasting our time. Sybil didn't have any.

"Anyway," she said, "I'm not too worried about it. If she gets caught in our net, we'll reel her in."

"What net?" I asked. "We have a net?"

She shrugged. "I heard that on the Cliché Channel. What time is it?"

"Eight forty," I said. "You can slow down. It's just on the next block."

Maizy swerved to a stop at the curb two doors down from Zara's. Ours was the only car on the street for the moment, but I could see people moving around inside, bringing the spa to life for the day.

I shrunk myself down inside my sweatshirt and crossed my arms. "We're going to talk to her before she goes in, right?"

Maizy glanced at me. "Why? Do these places intimidate you?"

My mouth twisted. "Of course not."

"Me, too," she said. We were quiet for a few minutes, watching the spa begin to breathe. "The blonde is really pretty," Maizy said softly.

I looked over at her, surprised. "You're really pretty, too, Maize."

She shrugged. Her eyes stayed on the spa. Mine stayed on her, but she didn't give anything away. Maybe I'd read too much into the comment.

"Here she comes," Maizy said a few seconds later. "Let's make sure we ask her about Bitsy Dolman."

We got out of the car and met Sybil on the sidewalk. She'd traded the red sequins for tailored white slacks, with a pale pink blazer, a chunky silver necklace and diamond stud earrings that flashed in the morning sun.

"Here." She thrust a piece of paper at me. "The guest list."

"I'll take that," Maizy said, and did, shoving it in her pocket.

"Let's make this fast," she said. "I don't want to be late."

I blinked. "You don't seem too upset over your husband's death."

"I'm a complete wreck over it." She inspected her nails. "You can't imagine my horror when I got home and found out."

Actually, I could imagine it, since Maizy and I had been the ones to find him in the first place, when we shouldn't have even still been there except for the fact that I hated to see all that filet mignon go to waste. Which explained why I currently had a freezer full of filet mignon purloined from a perfectly clean floor. And a purse that smelled like a stockyard.

She cocked her head at Maizy. "What's with the blue hair? Are you undercover?"

"If I was undercover," Maizy said, "I'd be a blonde."

"Got home from where?" I asked.

She seemed surprised. "We had a fight, remember? You were there. You know what happened. Everybody knows what happened."

"So where'd you go?" Maizy asked.

Sybil hesitated. "I had to get away for a while, so I went shopping."

Interesting choice of words: *had* to. As in *I had to get out of the house so my hired goon could kill my new husband?*

"Buy anything?" Maizy asked her.

She shook her head. "After an hour or so I calmed down and decided that wasn't the way I wanted to start my marriage. So I went home."

How convenient. No receipts.

"Where did you go?" I asked, thinking Maizy could hack into store security cameras for confirmation. I tried to remember what time everyone had disappeared after the food fight. Too late for a shopping excursion, unless Sybil shopped at a 24-hour Walmart. And I couldn't see *that* happening.

She shrugged. "Maxwell's. He opened the studio just for me."

I'd heard of Maxwell's. It was one of those private, appointment-only places that existed strictly for those lucky people who had too much money and not enough time to spend it.

"Did Oxnard swim?" Maizy asked abruptly.

Sybil blinked. "I have no idea."

Maizy was dug in. "How could you not know that?"

"I first went out with him in November," Sybil said, speaking very precisely, as if we were coming out of a deep anesthesia. "I married him in April. It wasn't swimming season."

"Why the rush?" Maizy asked. "Are you pregnant?"

Sybil glared at me. "Who is this person?"

I ignored that. "Tell us about Bitsy Dolman," I said.

"Bitsy Dolman." She tapped her finger to her chin. "Bitsy Dolman."

"Looks like Helen Mirren?" I prompted. "Sees the world through the bottom of a glass?"

She snapped her fingers, remembering. "I asked Oxie who she was and what she was doing on the guest list, and he said they went way back."

"They couldn't have been a couple," I said. "I mean, she must be twenty-five years younger than him."

"And how old do you think I am?" she snapped.

Oops.

"She's not his type," I said quickly. "I didn't know your husband very well, but he seemed to like his women...sober. I got the impression Bitsy used to live a much different life."

She shrugged. "He didn't speak much about her."

Something suddenly occurred to me. "But you must have known her. Bitsy claims she recommended Lizette Larue to you for your wedding."

She shook her head. "That's preposterous. Oxie recommended her."

"She was pretty clear that she'd spoken to you," I said.

"The way she drinks," Sybil said, "I doubt Bitsy is clear about anything."

Good point.

"What about his brother and sister?" Maizy asked. "Would they have reason to want Oxnard dead?"

To my surprise, Sybil burst into laughter, "Abigail is 92 and osteoporotic. She couldn't drown anything heavier than a cricket."

"But she could push a cricket into the pool," I argued. "Especially if that cricket had included her in his will."

Sybil gave a slow nod, conceding the point. "I don't know them that well, but Oxie always said he was just a bank account to Alston and Abby. She never worked a day in her life. And Alston...Alston had a rich brother." She glanced at her watch. "I'm going to be late for my appointment. Is there anything else?"

"Herman Kantz," I said. "How long have you known him?"

"Why would you ask that?"

"He told you to call him if you need him." I paused. "Why would you need him?"

Sybil shrugged. "Herman has a white knight complex. He was just being gallant if he said that."

"He said that," I told her.

There was a beat of silence.

"That's all I'm going to say about Herman Kantz," she said.

Maizy and I exchanged a glance.

"That's really all the time I have for this," Sybil said.

"We'll be in touch," Maizy told her. "We'll probably need to talk to you again."

"How I look forward to that." Sybil brushed past us and disappeared into the salon.

"I don't think she meant that," Maizy said. She checked the time on her cell phone. "I've got something to do. We'll visit Bitsy Dolman tomorrow. I'll pick you up at seven. I should probably mention the Z has a little brake problem. I might not be able to stop, but I'll be sure to slow down."

Oh, good. I could use some exercise.

* * *

Around six o'clock, while I was watching Animal Planet with Ashley and considering my dinner options, Curt knocked on the door holding a beer, a can of Coke, and a fat paper bag from Taco Bell. I answered it before realizing I was wearing a ratty T-shirt and baggy gray sweatpants with holes in the knees.

Either he didn't notice, didn't feel the need to comment, or didn't see the point since I'd always been happily unencumbered by fashion sense of any kind.

"So how was the wedding?" he asked when we'd settled in on the sofa. He passed me the Coke and a couple soft shell tacos. "Was it as bad as you thought?"

"It was *Animal House* in formal wear," I told him. I started eating the tacos out of the wrapper. "How'd it go at Cam's?"

He grimaced. "The question's how long it's gonna go. It's like he's building another house over there. We didn't even get it framed out yet."

"Maybe he should've hired a contractor," I said. "Are you any good at framing?"

"I'm good at everything," he said. "Now give me details."

I told him about the ceremony and the octogenarian food fight, leaving out the little factoid about the dead groom in the pool.

"Sounds interesting," he said when I was done. "Now are you going to tell me about the dead groom?"

"I want you to know I had nothing to do with it," I said immediately.

His eyebrow rose. "Nothing?"

I shook my head. That was my story and you know the rest of *that*.

He took a drink of beer. "You know, I was talking to Cam this morning. He mentioned that he thought Maizy might have sneaked out to meet up with a boyfriend last night. Said she didn't get home till almost two."

I chewed determinedly on my taco.

"I don't think Maizy has a boyfriend," he said. "Do *you* think she has a boyfriend?"

I swallowed. "Well, there's Brody Amherst."

"She thinks Brody Amherst is a putz," he said flatly.

From everything I'd heard about Brody Amherst, Maizy was right about that.

"You don't suppose she crashed the wedding, do you?" he asked. "Maybe made an anonymous call to the cops from a burner phone about 12:30 in the morning?"

"I was kind of busy," I said. "What with being the maid of honor and all."

"Yeah." He ran a hand over his hair with a sigh. "Listen, Jame, I know you and Maizy have the girl version of a bromance going on, but try to remember her father is a very large man and carries a gun."

As if I could forget. Every time I bought into one of Maizy's harebrained schemes, I was all too aware we were on dangerous ground if we happened to rattle past Cam Emerson in an Honest Aaron special.

CHAPTER EIGHT

———

At 6:59 Monday night, I was waiting on the curb when a rust-speckled green 240Z careened around the corner on two bald tires and slowed to about five miles an hour as it cruised down the block. I leaped up and made a run for it through a cloud of exhaust fumes. It took a couple of tries before I wrenched the door open and dove into the passenger seat, gagging.

Maizy shoved it into second gear, and we rocketed down the block, skulls glued to the headrests from the force. "So who's the office noob?"

Eunice? I looked at her. "How do you know about her? Did you cut school today?"

"I chose to abstain," she said. "Sitting too much is bad for you."

"So you decided to jog on over to Parker, Dennis, right?" I asked.

She shook her head. "I decided to *drive* over. Only I ran out of gas on account of the gauge must be broken. So I walked to the gas station. Exercise." She grinned at me. "So who's the noob?"

"Her name is Eunice Kublinski. She was hired last week," I said. "She just passed the Bar."

"That's cool," Maizy said. "Is she like Gloria Allred? Gloria Allred *rocks*."

I didn't see any Gloria Allred in Eunice. "Probably not," I said. "She seems kind of timid. And she went to Harvard Academy of Law and Mortuary Sciences online."

"Is that a real thing?" Maizy asked. "Cause if it is, I might want to check it out. I wouldn't mind knowing how to embalm someone."

I rolled my eyes.

"Knowledge is never wasted," she told me. "That's what my dad says. Of course, he also says I should take driver's ed. So you never know."

With Maizy at the wheel, it took about thirty seconds before we coasted to a stop in front of Bitsy Dolman's, a shabby split-level home in a shadowy cul-de-sac in Oakcrest. It had once been a decent neighborhood, but the '90s had been tough on local businesses and residents alike. It was a curious location that didn't square with her ritzy business address.

I'd read that the area was undergoing a resurgence, but you couldn't prove it from where I was sitting. The shutters were faded and peeling; the lawn was stippled with brown patches. Dead mums lurched from a plastic planter and collapsed to the ground. A decrepit canvas carport sagged in the driveway, putting a cap on the general sense of depression surrounding the place.

"This is nice," Maizy said.

Sure, if you were the Addams Family. I must have copied the address wrong. How could Bitsy live in a neighborhood like this?

We got out of the Z, sidestepping broken branches on the way up the weed-choked walk.

Bitsy came to the door on the third knock. Her gray wool slacks were stained, her purple silk blouse was wrinkled, and her eyes were sort of vacant, as if she wasn't quite there behind them. "Not interested," she said.

I tried to smile at her. "Aren't you Bitsy Dolman?"

"Who's asking?" She blinked and refocused. "You were at Oxnard's wedding."

"In the bridal party," I agreed.

"Bridal party." The words dripped disdain. "Don't even get me started." Her gaze shifted to Maizy. "Who're you?"

"Anastasia Thorpe," Maizy said. "Oxnard's granddaughter."

"Oxnard doesn't have a granddaughter," she said.

"I'm twice removed," Maizy said.

Bitsy frowned some more, as if she couldn't quite put that together.

A dog howled somewhere in the distance. Maybe a werewolf.

I cleared my throat. "May we come in?"

"If you feel you have to." She pushed the door open with her foot.

The inside was marginally better than the outside, but only because there were no weeds growing there. Lots of floral furniture and dated wallpaper, with a coating of filth over everything. I sat on the very edge of the sofa cushion while Maizy stood just inside the front door with an expression of horror.

Bitsy sat down, ankles crossed, back straight. A glass sat on the coffee table in front of her. There were circular water stains scattered like magic linking rings across the top of the table.

"So," she said. "Do you need a personal shopper?"

Of course I did. I mean, *look* at me, dressed like a thirteen-year-old boy without the style. But that was beside the point. I folded my hands piously, mostly because I didn't want to touch anything.

"Have you heard that Oxnard Thorpe passed away?" I asked gently.

Her eyes widened so dramatically that it was hard to tell if the reaction was genuine or a display for my benefit. "No, I—" She stopped, but her lips kept moving in little flutters with no sound. "Excuse me," she said faintly. She got up and left the room.

"She didn't ask what happened," Maizy whispered.

I nodded. *Everyone* asked what happened. Unless they already knew.

When Bitsy came back, she was clutching a green cashmere sweater tightly around herself as if to ward off a chill. "What happened?" she asked.

Maizy's lips twisted with disappointment.

"I'm sorry to say he was found dead in the swimming pool," I said carefully.

"Drowned?" Her voice was barely audible. She turned away, her hand pressed to her mouth. She seemed to be trying to gather herself.

I cleared my throat. "Would you mind if I ask where you went after his wedding reception?"

She turned back to me with a frown. "What?"

"I noticed you didn't stay long," I said. "Where did you go when you left?"

She picked up the glass. Her hand was steady. "Why? You just said he drowned in the pool."

Actually, I'd been careful *not* to say that.

"Marrying that woman was the silliest thing Oxnard ever did," she said. "I only attended for his benefit."

I figured as much. I also noticed she hadn't answered my question. "Had you known him long?"

A glimmer of a smile traced her lips. She wrapped her arms around herself, stroking the sweater absently. "Years. Since we were children, really. He was a dear friend."

"Did you approve of your friend marrying Sybil Sullivan?"

"It was none of my business." Her voice was firm. "I went to the wedding, and I left early for another social obligation."

I remembered her exit had been on the heels of Herman Kantz's exit. Probably Bitsy's social obligation had had to do with climbing.

I hesitated. "Bitsy, you didn't seem too impressed with Sybil and her friends."

"Friends." She snorted. "You mean employees. Don't even get me started on them."

Right. Clearly that angle was going nowhere.

"What sort of social obligation?" Maizy asked.

Bitsy looked up at her, startled. "I beg your pardon?"

"I bet you had a date with some guy you met online, right?" Maizy asked.

Bitsy went pale. "I most certainly did not. I attended a fashion show with my daughter."

Judging from her ensemble, she should've stayed a little longer. Except for the sweater, which was actually pretty nice, albeit mismatched. Maybe her stains and wrinkles were her version of dressing down after work.

"I've never been to a fashion show," I said, just to keep the conversation going.

"I'm not surprised." She took a slug from her glass. "The Fire and Ice show is elite. You wouldn't fit in."

I sensed a theme.

Finally she got around to the question I feared most. "Why are you so interested?"

I hesitated. "I've been hired to investigate Oxnard's death." In filet mignon. Otherwise we were doing this for Maizy's personal amusement.

"Oh," Bitsy said. "You have. And who might have hired you?"

"That's confidential."

"I thought so." She shook her head. "The widow Thorpe. I imagine she's busy redecorating Oxnard's mansion as we speak. She ought to be in jail," she muttered.

"Why do you say that?" Maizy and I asked simultaneously.

"Isn't it obvious?" She held her drink up, admiring the color. "She never loved him. She loved his money."

"How do you know that?" I asked.

"Everyone loved his money," Bitsy said.

"Did you?" Maizy asked. She glanced around. "'Cause it doesn't look like he gave you any."

"I'm redecorating," Bitsy said. "Open your eyes. Who else would kill a groom on his wedding night?"

That was one question, alright. But there was another.

"How well do you know the other wedding guests?" I asked.

Her mouth twisted. "I don't socialize with that element."

I was doing a stellar job of gathering information. I had no idea what to ask, no clue what Bitsy might be willing to talk about, nothing but instincts to go on. And my instincts were giving me zilch.

Fortunately, Bitsy didn't need much encouragement. "I do know Abby and Alston weren't happy when Oxnard took up with that gold digger."

Well, that was something. I nodded encouragingly. "Did they talk to you about that?"

Bitsy stared at me like I'd stolen her bourbon. "They didn't have to. They were raised on the *Main Line*, for God's sake. Sure, they've lived off their inheritance and then off their brother, but they know low class when they see it."

I'd heard of the Main Line. I wasn't exactly sure where it was, but I knew big money lived there.

Wait. Lived off their brother?

"But I suppose their troubles are over now," she said. "At least *someone's* troubles are over."

Was that a violin I heard?

She raised her glass in a toast. "Here's to Abby and Alston. May the silver spoons never fall out of their mouths." She took a nice long drink and belched behind her hand. "Oh, who'm I kidding? They've probably already started probating the will."

I'd just assumed Sybil had inherited everything, never thinking the Thorpe family also consisted of Stepford Thorpes. With all that money at stake, Oxnard's estate had all the makings of a court battle royale, and that was something Sybil would probably want to avoid.

And Sybil being in my life longer than necessary was something *I* wanted to avoid.

*   *   *

"What'd you think of her?" Maizy asked when we'd gotten back in the Z.

"I could see her pushing Oxnard in the pool," I said. "And the entire wedding party along with him. That is one bitter woman."

"I think she's sad and lonely." Maizy maneuvered around some fallen branches. "Her husband had a midlife crisis and ran off with a younger woman. Ow." She wiggled around in her seat. "Something's poking me."

Hopefully it wasn't breathing. "How could you possibly know that?" I asked.

She shrugged. "All men with midlife crises run off with younger women. It's in the handbook. My friend Belle? Her Uncle Billy quit the airline after thirty years, and now he teaches hula in Hilo with his twenty-year-old girlfriend." Her mouth twisted. "See what I mean? Sad. That's why Bitsy hoards things and drinks. Her husband's probably wearing a grass skirt and doing nicky-nack with some hot island babe."

I didn't know about that. If Curt showed up in a grass skirt, I wouldn't exactly have nicky-nack in mind. I'd have protective custody in mind.

"She was throwing serious shade at Sybil," I said.

"Maybe she had it bad for Oxnard," Maizy said. She shifted to one side, pulled something out of her back pocket, and dropped it on the dashboard. "His money made him a lot better looking than his looks did."

I stared at it. "Why'd you steal her electric bill, Maizy?"

"Because I want to know how bad her money problems are."

"And how do you know she's got money problems?"

Maizy glanced in the rearview mirror. "Because it's pretty dark back there, and her lights aren't on."

"Maybe she passed out on the sofa," I muttered.

"Maybe her utilities got turned off for nonpayment," Maizy said.

"Maybe the lights are on a timer," I said. "And they just haven't come on yet."

"Okay." Maizy swung over to the curb and let up on the gas. The Z coasted another ten feet before sagging to a stop. "Let's test that hypothesis."

We sat there in silence while full darkness enveloped the neighborhood. Plenty of mosquitoes. Some lightning bugs. No lights.

I scratched my arm. "I never said it was a hypothesis."

"So here's what I think." She started the car again. "Bitsy killed her dear old friend Oxnard because he refused to help her with her money problems after Mr. Bitsy took off on her."

"Or," I said, "He *wanted* to help her, but Sybil wouldn't let him. Maybe they had a fight about it, and Sybil killed him herself in a fit of rage." If only I'd been less concerned with salvaging dinner and more concerned with where the food fighters went.

"Or," Maizy said, "Alston and Abby killed him because he *was* helping her and spending their inheritance in the process."

"But where does Herman Kantz fit in?" I asked.

"It's a conundrum," Maizy agreed. She nodded at the utility bill. "You see why I wanted that?"

"Maybe we should take a peek at Oxnard's will," I said. "Find out who all the players are."

She snorted. "We could do that, but players change. Wills get contested all the time."

She was right there. Some of Howard's ugliest cases had involved heirs battling over an estate.

"Well," I said, "it can't hurt. We'll have a copy at the office. I'll look for it tomorrow."

"And I'll see if I can get Bitsy's lights turned on again," Maizy said. "Nobody should have to drink in the dark."

We were quiet for a few minutes while darkness slid past the window. I couldn't get past the feeling that something felt off about Bitsy. Well, pretty much everything felt off about Bitsy, but specifically her address. I dug into my purse until I found her business card. I'd remembered right; her office was on the main street of an upscale town a few miles away. It was possible that professional appearances were more important to her than living arrangements, but it seemed unlikely given what I now knew about Bitsy.

"Turn north on Merrick Highway," I said. "I want to check out Bitsy's office. From the outside," I added, before Maizy got any ideas.

"Cool. Why?"

"It doesn't add up," I said. "Why would she live in a ghost town and keep her business in Cedarwood?"

"Not enough money?" Maizy suggested.

"It's more than that," I said. "Her house was stuck in the '70s or something. You'd expect a personal shopper to have better taste. Or *some* taste."

"I see your point," Maizy said. "You think she's not what she seems to be."

It took fifteen minutes to get to Cedarwood, where we cruised slowly down Main Avenue beneath a sprawling canopy of leafy old maples and elms, past historic commercial buildings housing an ice cream parlor, a post office, a municipal building, and a quaint single screen movie theater with a marquee that read *African Queen*, all fronting onto a red brick sidewalk.

I consulted the card. "320 should be in the next block, up on the right. Maybe next to that real estate agent's office?"

We rolled past the real estate office while I gawked out the window, trying to read addresses or signs.

"320 is a dentist's office," Maizy said.

I rechecked the card. "It definitely says 320. Maybe she's on the second floor."

Maizy swerved over to the curb and bumped gently against it until the Z gave up and stopped in the vicinity of 320. The dentist's office was closed for the night, and the exterior sign didn't indicate any other businesses in the building.

"I don't get it," I said.

Maizy pulled out her cell phone and dialed the number on the card. After a few seconds, she said, "Not in service," and disconnected.

Huh.

"So Bitsy's handing out cards to a nonexistent business?" I asked. "Why would she do that? What are you doing?"

Maizy focused on the webpage she'd opened on her phone. "Not nonexistent. Defunct, for a year now." She dropped the phone into her pocket. "What does this tell us?"

"She's semi-retired," I said, "but maybe she's having a tough time making ends meet, so she still takes on work."

Maizy rolled her eyes. "Too pragmatic. What *else* does it tell us?"

I glanced at the dentist's office. "That it's time for a checkup?"

She shook her head. "It tells us that Bitsy lied to us, at least about this and probably about other things, too. Let's keep her on the list of suspects."

CHAPTER NINE

———

Early Tuesday morning, I pulled into the parking lot at Parker, Dennis to find a *blah* brown peanut with wheels— Eunice's peanut—parked in my spot at the far end of the lot, barely in sight of the office under a sap-spitting evergreen tree with a full complement of wild birds, each with an efficient digestive system and time to kill.

The peanut didn't move when I scowled at it. Although it may have trembled. I was pretty protective of my parking spot. I was lucky to have one. Wally had once tried to make the support staff walk to work to save parking for clients. If the best the clients could do was a Ford Legume, I didn't think parking spots were Wally's biggest problem.

I headed straight for the *T-Z* drawer in the file room to search for Oxnard's will. Uncomplicated matters like traffic tickets and wills were housed in thin manila folders, litigation files in fat expandable files. Both were mixed together and filed alphabetically. There was no Thorpe file. Which meant either that Howard kept it in his office, or he didn't keep a Thorpe file at all. It wasn't the first time he'd been unhelpful to me—the first time had been the day he hired me. I slid the drawer shut, disappointed.

Missy was nowhere in sight yet, but Eunice had plunked herself down at the empty secretarial desk across the room once occupied by an empty secretary named Paige Ford. Eunice blended into her environment well, wearing the same shade of brown as the desk. She'd lost the look of abject terror, so that was progress. She was frowning at a copy of the *New Jersey Law Journal*. I didn't see her turn one page in ten minutes, although her frown deepened. A few times, she got up for some coffee or a bathroom run. No calls came in for her, and when the mail came, none of that was for her, either.

I settled in to type Wally's new gem of a complaint. He was suing a range manufacturer, alleging its product was dangerous and defective because the burners actually got hot and Wally's client had given herself a second-degree burn trying to rearrange a teapot.

Even Gerber's would never bottle this pablum.

I sent it to the printer, thinking at least the unending flow of stupidity through the door kept me in Walmart purses, even if it put nothing in them. Then I improved my mood by taking another peek at Rod Rockstone. He was only getting better with age.

Around 11:15, after being summoned upstairs by Wally, Eunice came back juggling a fat manila file. She didn't notice the sheaf of papers that dropped out mid-juggle. Missing documents could mean legal malpractice, so I knelt to corral them back into place.

While I was on the floor, a pair of tasseled loafers appeared under my nose.

"I'd like to sue my parents," their owner said.

She was a starched white teenager wearing a starched white shirt, buttoned up to her lower lip, over a plain navy skirt. Brown hair shaped into an anchorwoman's bob around a heart-shaped face with an aggressively pert nose. Her eyes were large and green.

"Penny Dollarz," she said. She had a very firm handshake. "Emphasis on the *arz*." Everybody gets it wrong. Is there a lawyer in this place or what?"

Eunice didn't move. Worse than that, the terrified expression was back.

"There," I said, "is a lawyer."

Eunice blinked as if surprised by this.

"Meet Eunice Kublinski," I said.

Penny Dollarz turned to face her. "Can we talk privately in your office?"

"That is to say," Eunice said, although she hadn't actually said anything, "I don't really have…well, heretofore, subpoenas and habeas corpus—"

"Howard's office is free," I cut in before she wherefored Penny right out of the office.

"Yes," Eunice agreed. "Howard's office. Hold my calls." She circled Paige's desk, knocking Wally's file to the floor with her hip, to lead Penny upstairs.

Missy strolled in from the kitchen. "New client?"

I nodded. "Wants to sue her parents."

"A juvenile? Maybe you should have given it to Howard," Missy said. "That's complicated."

"Eunice will be fine. It'll give her something to do."

Missy sat down. "Speaking of something to do, did I tell you what Ryan and I did last weekend with a box of sponge cake and a bottle of baby oil?"

Luckily, the phone rang before she could launch into some Fun with Cake Mixes story.

Unluckily, it was my sister calling.

Sherri and I were nothing alike. She was tall and curvy, like my mother, while I was short and straight, like my father. She thrived on drama and chose her boyfriends accordingly. She lived for her wedding day and even worked in a bridal shop. And she'd once briefly dated Wally, leading him down a dark path into stick-on bunny tattoos and Sunrise Blonde hair dye. He'd pined for her from afar until he'd met a Mary Kay rep and turned in his tattoos and hair dye for bronzer and guyliner. Wally was highly impressionable.

"Kind of busy, Sher," I told her.

As usual, she ignored me. "I need your help. Can you pick up my prescription at the pharmacy and drop it off?"

I considered my stack of work. A request for production from Wally. Notices of deposition for Howard. A check from Ken payable to Sleepytime Mattresses to be mailed. Nothing that couldn't wait an hour. "Why can't you do it?" I asked. "Are you contagious?"

"No, I'm not contagious," she snapped. "I have poison ivy, if you must know."

"That's not exactly debilitating," I said. "You can't pick it up yourself?"

Moment of silence.

"I can't sit in the car," she said. "I can't sit *anywhere*. Frankie thought it would be fun to do it in the woods and—"

It was turning out to be one of those days.

CHAPTER TEN

———

     I snarfed down my lunch in ten minutes and drove to the pharmacy in two, trying to squeeze Sherri's mission of mercy within my allotted twenty-minute lunch hour. I wasted eight more minutes standing in line, and when I got to the counter, her prescription wasn't ready, so I took a seat in the waiting room in view of the television tuned to a cooking show. The chef was whipping up one of those meals that amounted to a tablespoon of food swimming in a half gallon of sauce. Much ado about nothing, if you asked me. He followed that up with dessert, some kind of frilly bite-sized thing. Before I knew it, I was absorbed in the intricacies of something called crème patisserie when I heard the raised voices coming from the head of one of the pharmacy line.

     "You don't understand," a feeble male voice was saying. "We can't afford that."

     The pharmacist said something that I couldn't hear.

     "Please," an equally feeble female voice implored, "Don't you offer senior discounts?"

     I felt a stab of sympathy until I turned my head to see that it was Abigail and Alston Thorpe standing at the counter pleading poverty. What kind of scam were they running? Playing it cool, I rotated in the seat until I was facing the counter instead of the TV, which meant I was then nearly straddling the chair backwards. Which was quite hard to do without ramming my knee into the adjacent chair, and I did nothing the easy way. My kneecap hit the thing so hard, I practically shoved it across the room, screeching the whole way on the tile floor. But I reacted with great poise and dignity.

     "Dammit!" I howled.

Across the room, a little girl with her right arm in a half cast watched me with silent fascination, the way kids will do. Her mother watched me with horror.

Fortunately, my covert investigative skills paid off. The Stepford Thorpes looked nothing like they had at Oxnard's wedding. Alston was wearing a University of Pittsburgh sweatshirt with tomato sauce stains on it and tan trousers that were shiny in the seat. Abigail had made more effort but to less effect. Her black pantsuit might have been stylish in its day, but its day had passed two decades ago, and now it was just old and threadbare. Her shoes were black patent without most of the shine, wear spots on the sides and white showing at the heels.

Alston had his arm around her thin shoulders and at the same time was clearly trying to summon the days of yore when he'd been stronger and more intimidating. And richer. Had I heard correctly, they had no money to pay for their prescription? How could it be possible that the Thorpe twins had no money when they were both, well, Thorpes?

Fortunately, they were so intent on their own duplicity, neither one had heard me.

"There are some programs," the pharmacist was telling them. "But you're not enrolled in any of them. Your balance is $289."

Abigail and Alston stared at each other in mutual uncertainty. Abigail's lip trembled like she was going to cry. I almost felt like crying watching them. Part of me wanted to run up to them waving the $289 they needed. Another part of me wanted to crawl under my chair in shame because I didn't have $289 on me. Or at home. Or in the bank.

"Move aside, please," the clerk said. "There are people waiting."

They took a simultaneous step away from the counter, still clinging to each other, and headed for the exit, Abigail sniffling and Alston fuming in the kind of impotent fury only bureaucracy can foment.

"That is so wrong," a woman across the room said, watching them. "That poor couple. I'm never getting old."

Yeah. Good luck with that.

I looked after the Stepfords, torn. Then I glanced at the pharmacist, who didn't seem to be waving me over to pick up my sister's prescription. I looked at the little girl, who was still staring at me, but with less fascination now that I'd quieted down. And then I did the only thing I could think to do.

I got up and followed the Thorpes.

CHAPTER ELEVEN

———

Which got me nowhere. They walked in lockstep to an old dented four-door Chevy Gargantuan, the official car of senior citizens everywhere, and sat there in the parking lot, probably trying to figure out how to raise $289 without selling a kidney. I sat in my car ten minutes waiting for something more interesting to happen. It didn't. I started the car and drove back to work.

By the time I got to the office, Eunice was nowhere in sight, which was a good sign, but Missy was frazzled, which was not. She shoved a stack of papers at me. "Take these to Eunice right away. I have people on hold."

I took the steps two at a time and burst into Howard's office. Eunice's head snapped up from a yellow legal pad where she'd been scribbling furiously.

I closed the door. "What can I do?"

"I've been gathering information," Eunice said. "For Miss Dollarz's file. I think it's a good case. Improper imposition of curfew."

"Curfew?" I repeated.

She nodded. "It'll set legal precedent. I'm laying the groundwork. See?" She pointed to the legal pad. Name, address, yes, fine, Social Security number, okay.

I blinked. "Astrological sign?"

"You never know what may be pertinent in a lawsuit," Eunice said.

"I'm a Scorpio," Penny Dollarz said helpfully.

"We might even have a class action on our hands," Eunice added. "Wouldn't that be something?" She beamed at Penny. "That would be something."

I didn't even think we had a case on our hands as I ran down the rest of the personal information. Model and year of car.

Pierced ears. Pet calico cat named Loveycakes. "Eunice," I began.

Wally stuck his head into the room. "I thought I might be of some help. Melissa told me we have a new client."

Wally's idea of help was to whisk Penny out from under Eunice's nose.

"We have things under control," I said.

Wally glanced at Penny. She stared straight ahead like she'd just been Tased.

"It's a troubling case," I said.

"Troubling," Eunice agreed. "But with great potential."

Wally crossed his arms. "Tell me about it."

"Improper imposition of curfew." She beamed at him. "We could have a class action suit. All those teenagers with unjust curfews."

Wally's arms fell to his sides. "Improper…?"

"The phone will be ringing off the hook," she said. We all looked at the phone, sitting on the desk with its mouth shut. "Before long," she added.

Wally stared at me. I stuck my face in the papers that formed the foundation of a file. The papers Eunice should have had with her when she sat down with Penny.

"Just a few minutes more," I said. "We just need the contingent fee agreement."

"Contingent fee agreement," Eunice agreed.

Wally's face brightened. The CFA spelled out precisely how much money the firm stood to earn on any recovery in the case.

Eunice pushed the paper across the desk along with a neon green hexagonal pen that read *Bruno's Deli—We Got Your Hot Salami Right Here*. Penny picked it up with great distaste, signed her name, and pushed it back to Eunice, blushing faintly.

"And the releases," I said, shoving more papers at Eunice.

"The releases," she agreed, shoving them at Penny.

Wally backed out, shaking his head like a bug had just flown into his ear. I had to give him credit for holding it together in front of the client, but that composure couldn't last. He was going to unload on Eunice sooner or later.

"What's a release for?" Eunice whispered at me.

I turned to Penny. "It allows us to get any personal information we need like medical records, tax returns, things of that sort."

"I don't file taxes," she told me. "I'm seventeen."

"Medical records, then."

"I haven't seen any doctors."

"Just sign them, dear," I said tightly.

She did, clearly unconvinced about the whole thing. "How long before something happens?"

Eunice looked up at me. Seemed she had all the answers as long as there were no questions.

"Hard to say," I said. "Depends on what kind of response we get and how fast."

"You never know," Eunice added. "Until you know."

Frowning, Penny gathered up her tiny handbag, slung it across her body, passed out bone-crushing handshakes, and disappeared in a fog of confusion.

"That went pretty well, I think." Eunice fanned herself with the CFA. "What do you think?"

"Are you sure you're up for this case?" I asked.

"Oh, sure. It's just nerves. This is all so new." She flapped the CFA harder. "Is it hot in here? Am I flushed?"

Just as soon as Wally talked to Howard, she was.

I printed *Dollarz, Penny* on a file folder. "Didn't they teach you about fee agreements and releases in law school?"

"I guess not." She felt her forehead. "I might faint. Is there a defibrillator nearby?"

Geez. "Just stay here and relax," I told her. "Howard won't need his office for a while."

"I was so keyed up about getting this job, I stayed awake most of last night," she said. "I could use a nap."

At least it would keep her away from the law journals that were giving her crazy ideas.

* * *

"Are you avoiding me?" I asked Janice an hour later. "You didn't show up yesterday." We were in her office, which was not a comfortable place. On the small side, plain white walls, bare floor, white mini blinds drawn up to the top edge of the single window, and a computer with an enormous flat panel monitor which enabled her to keep the firm's accounts straight while simultaneously keeping track of her latest eBay bid.

"Of course I am," she said. "You terrify me."

I knew sarcasm when I heard it. I narrowed my eyes at her. "You didn't say anything about being the maid of honor."

She glanced up from her monitor with a mixture of irritation and mild surprise. "I didn't know."

"I don't believe you," I said. "Do you have any idea what I went through? I have bruises on my backside from the groom!"

"Oh, yeah." She shrugged. "He does that."

"Little correction," I snapped. "He *used* to do that. He's dead."

"Then you'd better tell Howard," she said. "He'll want to get his final bill submitted to the estate."

Janice's milk of human compassion had turned sour a long time ago.

"Don't you want to know what happened?" I asked.

With a sigh, she yanked off her reading glasses. "Did you kill him?"

"Of course not!"

"Then I don't need to know," she said. She chewed thoughtfully on the arm of her glasses. "Although that is a big hit to the revenue stream. He was good for a few specious lawsuits a year." She shrugged. "Oh, well. There'll be another litigious old lizard out there."

"I want my five hundred dollars," I said through gritted teeth.

Her attention was back on the monitor. "Be serious. You didn't actually believe that, did you?"

Actually, I had. *Why* had I believed that? Janice wouldn't be honest about the time of day if it didn't suit her purposes. Still, I resorted to the time-honored argument of the nine-year-old. "But you promised!"

She blew out a disdainful snort. "You don't really think I'm going to embezzle for you."

I pointed at the window behind her. "Let's talk about embezzling. Are we supposed to believe you can afford that on your salary?"

We looked out at the branches of a leafy oak tree. Her office was on the second floor.

Janice shrugged again. "Believe what you want. You've got nothing on me. The wedding's over. Maybe you should have taken a little memento while you had the chance."

"Steal from a dead man?" I practically yelled. "Do you have *any* ethics?"

"He wasn't dead when you got there," she said. "Was he?"

That was open for debate. But I knew a losing argument when I fought one, so I flung the door open and went back to work.

CHAPTER TWELVE

———

"You can't be serious," Curt said.

It was nearly nine o'clock Thursday night and we were sitting on my sofa, plump and lazy after a takeout spaghetti dinner. The Phillies were on television. A light rain had started to fall outside. Ashley was curled up in Curt's lap asleep. Life was good. I'd even managed to avoid explaining Maizy's last failure to launch at the DMV through the tactical use of changes of subject and bogus migraines ever since. Until my creativity and Curt's patience had run out. Of course, I'd left out the part about the door and the examiner falling off and out respectively. I'd sort of substituted an engine problem in a car borrowed from a friend. You know, for reality.

"Don't be too hard on her," I said. "She's already been blacklisted for three months."

"Then she should have borrowed a reliable car," he said. "What was she thinking?"

I shrugged. "Who knows how Maizy's mind works. She could have done something worse." Like doctor up a phony license.

Curt stared grimly at the TV. "I know."

"And she can always reschedule," I said. *Again.*

"I know," he said.

"You're mad," I said. I could tell, by the tense set of his jaw and the hard line of his lips. Also the way his eyebrows were practically sitting on his cheeks.

His chest heaved in a sigh. "Not mad. Disappointed. I'd like to give her the Civic before it becomes an antique." His dimple flashed. "Speaking of antiques, I saw a story on the news about Oxnard Thorpe's death. Interesting guy."

Someone knocked on my door, saving me from an awkward confession about investigating that death. Curt didn't exactly approve of me playing detective. He didn't approve of me seeing dead people, either, especially since I saw them for real. Still, he kept hanging in there, which went to show he was more than just a pretty face on top of a smoking hot body with a killer sense of humor and a fierce protective streak. Like that wasn't enough.

Another knock.

"Hold that thought," I told him, and got up to find Maizy standing on the landing, holding a bulging backpack.

"I've got a plan," she told me. "I'm sleeping over 'cause we've got to get an early start."

I stepped outside. "This might be a bad time, Maize. You should've called."

"I called your cell," she said. "You should've answered."

"My cell's not on," I said.

She rolled her eyes. "It's never on. Do you get the concept of a cell phone?"

Sure. They were a convenience for telemarketers intent on harassing me.

"Curt's here," I said. "We were talking about..." I drifted off, not wanting to embarrass her.

I should've known better.

"So I'm temporarily blacklisted," she said. "Big deal. A license is only a bribe so the state will let me do something I'm already doing for free. By the way, Honest Aaron fixed the brakes on the 240Z on account of I'm such a good customer, so it can stop now."

"Did he fix the seat, too?"

"Baby steps," she said. "He's a busy man. So check this out." She held up a phony license. There was that ghastly zombie apocalypse photo seen on licenses everywhere, only this one was of Maizy. There was the red New Jersey lettering. She'd even laminated it.

"This is *so* not a good idea, Maize," I told her. I looked closer. "How'd you do the watermarks?"

She shrugged. "I didn't. Brody Amherst's sister April works at the DMV. I gave her everything and she took care of it for twenty bucks. Now that that's out of the way, we have a reason to go talk to the walking dead."

"And who might that be?" Curt asked from behind me. He was in the doorway, arms crossed, glowering at us. It was a good look for him. It shaded his brown eyes almost black and showed off his biceps. I should make him glower more often. Shouldn't be that hard to do.

"It's a new exhibit at the Franklin Institute," Maizy said without hesitation. "It's pretty cool, Uncle Curt. They've got zombies walking around. You know, mingling."

"Why don't you come in out of the rain and tell me about it," he said. "I might want to go with you."

Maizy shot me a sidelong glance as she dropped her backpack in my tiny foyer. We followed Curt into the living room. Maizy picked up Ashley and sat in the recliner. Curt and I reclaimed our seats on the sofa. The baseball game had been muted. Outside, the rain had gotten a little heavier.

"Help me out," Curt said when we were settled in. "What does April Amherst at the DMV have to do with a zombie exhibit at the Franklin Institute?"

"She sold me passes," Maizy said. "Through Brody."

His expression didn't change. "That was nice of her. Can I see them?"

"I have to pick them up in the morning," Maizy said. "She didn't have them on her at work."

Curt glanced at me. I kept my mouth shut.

After a few seconds, he sighed. "I'm getting a bad feeling here."

"It's probably the spaghetti," Maizy said, gesturing to the remnants of our dinner. "Jamie's not a very good cook."

"Hey," I said, "it was takeout!"

Ashley lifted her head and stared at me. Like she would know. As long as her Meow Mix and treats kept flowing, I was Emeril Lagasse to her.

"You're doing it again," Curt said. "Aren't you?"

"Define *it*," Maizy said.

His lips pressed together hard. "You're trying to find out who killed Oxnard Thorpe," he said. "Despite the fact you could have both been killed three times over pretending to be the Dynamic Duo."

"There's no pretending here," Maizy said. "We're awesome."

I grinned. I kind of had to agree with her. Maybe we weren't detectives in the traditional sense—okay, no *maybe* about that—but we'd gotten the job done more than once in the past, so that had to count for something.

Curt sat back. "Okay, what've you got so far?"

Maizy and I glanced at each other.

"Either you tell me," he said, "or I make sure Cam grounds you until your thirtieth birthday."

Maizy opened her mouth.

"And nails your bedroom window shut," Curt added. "And makes you wear a GPS."

Ashley looked at him with alarm.

Maizy closed her mouth.

"There's no need for strong-arm tactics," I told him. "We only talked to the bride and one of the wedding guests, and she kind of pointed the finger…well…" I hesitated, remembering Bitsy's equal opportunity hostility.

"She pointed fingers everywhere," Maizy said. "We're just following up."

"Starting with the walking dead," Curt said. "And who exactly might that be?"

"Oxnard's brother and sister," I said. "I don't really see them killing him since they could barely throw a salad, but money does funny things to people. Although it turns out they aren't rich. They didn't even have $289 to pick up a prescription."

"That's interesting," Maizy said. "Guess Moneybags Oxnard didn't like to share the wealth."

"It was sad, actually," I said, thinking about it. "They were really upset."

Curt frowned. "Wait a minute. Throw a salad?"

"It's a long story," I said.

"No, it's not," Maizy said. "The rich people had a food fight at the wedding. Which was really convenient, because nobody noticed that I left."

He stared at her. "Why were *you* there?"

"I wasn't," she said. "I just told you, I left."

He sighed and pushed both hands through his hair. "I know there's no stopping you," he said finally. "Would you at least try to be sensible about this? And give me a heads up next time you want to go talking to zombies so I can go with you."

"We'll be fine," I said. "They're pretty old. We can outrun them if they come after us."

Maizy nodded. "Or at least walk faster," she said.

CHAPTER THIRTEEN

———

When I was nine, I caught the flu and the chicken pox at the same time and spent the better part of a week getting to know myself inside and out.

It had still been better than sharing a bed with Maizy. She shoved, kicked, and elbowed her way through the night, and when I was good and tenderized, she spooned me until 6:30 came. By then I'd had enough of everything but sleep, so I got up to get dressed.

I wasn't a morning person even when *morning* meant 7:30. At 6:30, after about two hours of sleep and six hours of defending myself, I felt dizzy and disoriented. The pattern on the carpet seemed to be swimming across the floor, and I very nearly saw two reflections of myself in the bathroom mirror, which horrified me into a different level of consciousness immediately. I think they call it shock.

"I've been thinking," Maizy said from behind me.

I don't know when she'd found the time, what with the four straight hours of Tae Bo.

"Maybe we should stop for doughnuts," she said. "Old people like doughnuts, right?"

I spun around to face her. "You want to bribe them with doughnuts?"

"That's a good idea," she said. She stuck both hands in her hair, ruffled it around some, and pulled them out. Her hair stayed poofed. She glanced at her reflection, nodded once, and walked away.

Show-off.

I had just given up trying to de-frizz and was going for the ever popular ponytail when I heard a knock on my door and the sound of Maizy answering it. Probably Curt. Maybe he'd called in sick so that he could join us. That would be alright with me. Things tended to go more smoothly when Curt was along. Plus he was fun to look at.

Except that wasn't Curt's voice I heard. It was—

"I'm Eunice Kublinski," the voice said. "I work with Jamie. I'm a lawyer."

"Do you like it?" Maizy asked.

"Not so much," Eunice admitted. "I'm not very good at it."

"It's boring, right?" Maizy said. "Maybe I can help. I'm really smart."

I practically ran out of the bathroom before Maizy could help. "Eunice! What are you doing here?"

She gave a start. "I know it's early, but I kind of wanted to talk to you outside of the office. I didn't expect you to have company."

"I took a vacation day, anyway," I said.

"And I'm not company," Maizy told her. "I'm her partner. We're detectives."

Eunice's jaw went slack.

My smile was shaky. "Maizy is kind of a comedian. You never know what she's going to say."

"Oh." She nodded. "I see. Heh heh."

"Not everyone gets me," Maizy said. "I'm an enigma."

"I wish I was an enigma," Eunice said. "I'm just a bad lawyer."

"You don't know that," I told her, although I had my doubts.

"Thing is," she went on, "I thought it'd be easy. Being a lawyer."

"Yeah." Maizy nodded. "Same with the detective thing. It's really something how much planning goes into it. It's exhausting."

"It's all in the details," Eunice said. "Lawyers call it *minutiae*."

"That's a good word," Maizy said. "It's the *minutiae* for me, too."

"That's funny," Eunice said. "For you I'd think it'd be the hair."

Maizy blinked. "What about it?"

"You're kidding, right?" Eunice said. "It's blue. And it's..." She held both arms up in a halo shape. "...*big*."

"She means memorable," I said quickly. "But not in a bad way."

"Well, not in a good way, either," Eunice said. "For a detective, I mean. You need to tone it down. You want to blend."

Well, I had to admit, she was an expert at blending. Right now she was blending into my beige carpet. All except for her mouth.

"This is my mojo," Maizy said, unperturbed. "I don't mess with my mojo."

"Well, your mojo makes you stand out in a crowd," Eunice said. "That's not good for a detective. I'm just saying. As a lawyer."

"What do you want, Eunice?" I asked. "We're getting ready to go somewhere."

"I need some advice," she said. "Wally told me the Dollarz case is a no-go, but I think that's sour grapes because it's *my* case. And I want to pursue it. After all, men can be as aggressive as they want to be, and no one thinks less of *them* for it. But I'm supposed to scale it back."

"She's got a point," Maizy told me.

"I know she's got a point," I snapped. "But there's nothing I can do about it."

"You could take me with you," Eunice said. "I could learn a lot from you two. I won't say anything, I promise."

"I don't think that's a good idea," I said.

"Good idea," Maizy said at the same time. "It might be handy to have a lawyer with us."

Eunice brightened. "Where are you going? Are you detecting something?"

I was detecting something, alright, and it had nothing to do with Oxnard Thorpe's demise. Including Eunice in a road trip to the Stepford Thorpes sounded like a very bad idea. "I don't know," I said doubtfully. "We kind of work alone."

"I won't get in the way," Eunice said. "I'll just watch and be quiet. I won't say a word."

"Don't worry about that," Maizy said. "They probably won't hear you anyway. They're old."

"I worry all the time," Eunice told her. "About everything."

"Well," Maizy said, "life's a burden."

Eunice frowned at us.

"You can never be sure," I told her.

Forty minutes later, we drove through the gates of the Golden Leaves Over-55 Community and parked in front of a minuscule house with white siding, blue shutters, a blue front door, and a strip of grass for a lawn. Every house in the community was minuscule with white siding and blue shutters, a blue front door, and a strip of grass for a lawn. Every window showed white blinds or white drapes. No trash cans in sight. No cars parked in the street. No fences.

"This isn't anything like those senior living commercials," Maizy said. "I can see why they'd want to kill Oxnard. Just being near all this conformity is making me hostile."

"It's not *that* bad," I said. "At least everything's clean."

"So's an operating room," she said. "But I wouldn't want to live there."

"Is this about Oxnard Thorpe?" Eunice asked from the back seat. "I read about that. Are you investigating that?"

"We're detectives, aren't we?" Maizy said.

No answer. Eunice wasn't convinced.

We got out of the car, Eunice holding the box of doughnuts. The lid was popped open. Eunice had powdered sugar around her mouth.

"I hope you don't mind," she said. "I eat when I'm nervous."

I lifted the lid. She'd eaten four doughnuts.

"Try to calm down," I told her.

She nodded and took a deep breath. "I really need to talk to you," she whispered.

Maizy was halfway up the immaculate walk. "Come on, you guys," she called back. "We have to catch them before their naptime."

I rolled my eyes and followed her. "Behave yourselves," I warned them. "This shouldn't take long."

I could hear faint strains of Frank Sinatra inside when I knocked on the door.

Abigail Thorpe opened the door, even smaller and more wrinkly close up, with dark shadows under her eyes and a slackness to her mouth that spoke of exhaustion. She had a cast on her left wrist, bearing her brother's signature in spidery handwriting and a gold star sticker which for some reason I found touching.

She frowned when she saw me standing there, the way you do when you suspect you've met someone before, couldn't quite place them, and didn't really care to try. In the background, Sinatra was telling someone she'd be easy to love.

I stepped in front of Maizy and Eunice. "Miss Thorpe, my name is Jamie Winters. I was at your brother's wedding. I'm so sorry for your loss. Oxnard was"—a creep—"a fine man."

She squinted at me. "What's that?"

Worth a try. "I'm working for his wife," I said.

"Martha?" she screeched.

I shook my head. "No, I mean—"

"Anna?"

Another head shake. "No, Miss Thorpe, I mean—"

"Rosemarie?"

Oh, for Pete's sake.

"Sybil," I said. "Sybil Sullivan Thorpe."

"Oh. *Her.*" Abigail's wrinkles puckered. "She's a low-class moneygrubber. She never loved my brother."

That seemed to be the popular opinion.

"Why do you say that?" Maizy asked.

Abigail's eyes cut to her. "She wanted his money. And his house. *My* house. And I wouldn't put it past her to kill him to get it."

My house? Abigail might be small and weak, but she had a mean streak and a motive.

"How did you hurt your wrist?" I asked her, envisioning her shoving Oxnard into the pool in a fit of pique over his marrying Sybil and depriving her of her inheritance.

She glanced at the cast. "I was rolling out cookie dough."

With what? A cinderblock?

"I like cookies," Eunice said. "Especially chocolate chip cookies."

"Have a doughnut," I whispered. I turned to Abigail. "Can we talk? I'm looking into Oxnard's passing."

"And sugar cookies," Eunice said. "I like sugar cookies. And gingerbread."

So much for keeping her mouth shut.

I sighed. "Do you remember where you and your brother went last Saturday night after the ceremony?"

"I don't understand," Abigail said. "Why are you asking *me*? Do you think I had something to do with this? Why are you accusing me?"

Until the *my house* comment, I hadn't thought so. Now I wasn't so sure.

"Yes," Eunice whispered, elbowing me in the ribs. "Why?"

"Why is a good question," I agreed. "Why do you think Oxnard's death wasn't accidental?"

"I have my reasons," Abigail told me. "That dreadful woman had reasons to want my brother dead. You'll see." She narrowed her eyes at me. "Who are you to be asking these questions?"

Another good question.

"Who are you again?" she asked, her voice sharpening.

Eunice stepped forward to slap a business card into Abigail's good hand. "Eunice Kublinski, Esquire. Personal injury, wills and estates, improper imposition of curfew."

Good grief.

"A lawyer?" A smile stitched itself into Abigail's creases and folds. "You must be here to discuss the will." She turned and yelled, "Alston! Oxnard's lawyers are here!"

"No, we—" I began, but then Alston appeared, peering at us through thick black glasses. He was wearing khaki pants, a gray cardigan buttoned to his neck, and Nikes. The cardigan had a hole in the left elbow and the pants were dirty at the knees.

Frank Sinatra informed us it was quarter to three and there was no one in the place. I wished I was living in his world.

Abigail pointed at us. "Look, Alston, it's..." She faltered. "I'm sorry. I've forgotten your names." Interesting. She'd been in command until her brother had shown up, and suddenly she was feeble and uncertain. I didn't buy it.

"Eunice Kublinski," Eunice said, honing in on Alston with a vigorous handshake. "Attorney," she added. "My card." She whipped out another business card.

Where had the real Eunice gone?

I reached for Alston's hand. "I don't know if you remember me but—"

"You stood for *her,*" he said with disgust.

How could he have remembered me? No one ever remembered me. Especially when I was in the orbit of people like Dusty Rose.

"I'm sorry for your loss," I said again. "May I talk to you for a few minutes?"

"About what?"

"We brought you doughnuts." Eunice shoved the box at him.

He lifted the lid. "There are no chocolate jimmies in here."

I frowned at Eunice.

"Chocolate jimmies are my favorite," she whispered.

Maizy grinned. As usual, she was having fun. She was also being suspiciously quiet. She was up to something, or soon would be. I knew the signs.

"Alston!" Abigail swatted him out of the way. "Don't be rude. The lawyers have come to tell us what we've inherited. Come right in." She took my arm and pulled me across the threshold. Eunice followed after a slight hesitation. Maizy skipped behind us like she had entered the gates of Disney World.

Abigail led us to a blinding sitting room with white drapes, white furniture, white floor, and a small electric fireplace. Through a rectangular cutout on the far wall, a galley kitchen was visible. A hallway branched off to our right with more white tiles and three closed doors.

Abigail dispatched Alston for tea and cookies and arranged herself onto one of the overstuffed chairs. I got the distinct feeling she was anything but fragile. But was she strong enough to shove Oxnard into the pool? Of course she was. Oxnard's own best days had been nearly a century ago.

"You must forgive Alston," she said. "It's been a trying few days. It's such a tragedy when one is taken so young."

Maizy snorted. I gave her a pointed scowl and she shrugged.

"Is that a real fireplace?" Eunice asked.

"Is that a Sony?" Maizy asked. "I bet *Big Bang* kills on that."

Abigail blinked and looked my way. Why did everyone do that?

Alston returned holding a tray with a teapot and mismatched cups and a plate of Lorna Doones. I was struck by his command of the room, even at his age. He must have been something in his younger days.

Eunice floated over to the teapot while Maizy stood beside me with her hands in her pockets, head cocked to the side, appraising the Stepford Thorpes as if she'd never seen old people before.

Abigail waited until her brother had poured tea and offered cookies. Maizy snatched up a half dozen cookies, stuffing them in her pockets, and drifted into the background.

"So about my brother's will," Abigail said. "He left us his house, didn't he?"

"Don't be crass, Abby." Alston settled in with a cup of tea.

"It should be ours," she shot back. "That vile woman shouldn't get a dime. She's stealing from us. That's *our* money."

I had to hand it to her. I didn't think I could talk back to Alston Thorpe. It only solidified my suspicion that Abigail was steelier than she seemed.

"Can I use your bathroom?" Maizy asked suddenly. Alston pointed and she galloped away.

"Oxnard was so proud of his house," Abigail told us. "He earned every brick of it. Do you know he started a lemonade stand one summer while all the other six-year-olds were frittering away their days playing?"

Slackers.

"He made eighty dollars that summer. What a head for business." Her expression hardened. "Of course, that was before he forgot what family means. The fool."

Oh, boy. I got the feeling Abigail's definition of *family* involved the transfer of money. I wondered when Oxnard had moved from lemonade into adult diapers. Not important. I still knew nothing I hadn't already known except that the Stepford Thorpes lived in Sterility City and success had gone to Oxnard's head. Big surprise.

I suddenly realized Maizy was still gone.

Eunice cleared her throat and tipped her head the tiniest bit in the direction of the hallway. One of the three doors was slightly ajar. Well, that was just great. Now we'd have to keep Alston distracted so that Maizy didn't get caught. I wasn't good at calm distraction.

"Where did you go after the ceremony?" I blurted.

See?

Abigail blinked, her rose-tinted reverie interrupted. "What does that have to do with our inheritance?"

"Just part of the process," I said.

"Process," Eunice agreed.

"What would the world do without its paperwork?" I added.

"Paperwork," Eunice agreed with a "what can you do?" shrug. I was starting to wish she'd pass out again.

"I don't understand," Alston said.

I opened my mouth to answer, but Eunice beat me to it. "In order to open probate, we just need a bit of information for our files. It will make everything move more smoothly in the end. *Res ipsa loquitur.*"

I was pretty sure she had no idea what that meant.

"Oh," Abigail said. "Of course." She nibbled on a cookie and thought. "Well, I can't say I remember exactly where...do you remember, Al?"

"We came home," Alston said flatly. "We watched the news and went to bed." He looked steadily at his sister. "Don't you remember?"

"Oh," she said again. "Oh, yes. Of course." She smiled at Eunice. "Does that help?"

"Was it just the two of you?" I cut in. "Did you have any of the guests staying with you?"

"It was," Alston said, "just the two of us. I hardly see why that matters."

A little thing called alibi. I stood and Eunice leaped to her feet beside me. "Thanks for your time," I said. "We'll be in touch."

"But I want to know about our inheritance," Abigail said.

"We'll make sure you get everything that's coming to you," Maizy told her. I hadn't even seen her come back. She beamed at me.

I knew that smile. It meant that things were about to get worse.

CHAPTER FOURTEEN

———

"You have to stop doing that," I told Maizy when we got back in the car.

"What?" she asked innocently. "Doing good deeds and spreading sunshine?"

I rolled my eyes. "Yeah," I said. "That."

"You wouldn't say that if you knew what I found." She held up a pink glob.

"What's that?" I asked.

"That," Maizy said, "is a detective's best friend. Well, next to his gun. And his surveillance equipment. And his handcuffs. And maybe his stun gun. And a good telephoto lens."

Probably all those things were in my trunk at that very moment. Maizy had a habit of using my trunk as her personal armory. I never knew what she'd stashed in there. Served me right for not cleaning out my car more often.

I caught a familiar scent when she waved the glob in my face. "That's Play-Doh," I said.

"I love Play-Doh," Eunice said. "Can I have a sniff?"

Maizy stuck her arm between the seats. Eunice practically stuck her nose in the glob, sucked in a giant breath, closed her eyes, and said, "Mmm."

"I know what you mean," Maizy told her. She took a big whiff and held it out to me.

I pushed it away. "And this helps us how?" I asked. "Abigail probably uses it for therapy."

"*I* use it for impressions," she said. She shoved the pink glob in front of my eyes to show me the distinct impression of a key. "Can we stop at a hardware store?" she asked. "I want to get a key made."

"That doesn't sound legal," Eunice asked.

"Of course it is," Maizy said. "People get keys made all the time. It's only illegal if I use it to break and enter. Of course, if I have a key, I'll only be entering, right?"

I glanced at Eunice in the rearview mirror.

"That sounds right," she said, nodding.

"How do you know it's the key to their house?" I asked.

"Keen intuition," Maizy said. "Also, they had all their keys hanging on hooks and labeled. This isn't rocket science."

Especially the way we did it.

"I hate to disappoint you," I said, "but we're not going to break into the Thorpes' house."

Maizy rolled her eyes. "Did you forget already? It's not *breaking* if I have a key."

"*I* didn't forget," Eunice said. "I've got a really good memory."

"Don't help her," I said. "We have no reason to go back there."

"Yeah, you're right," Maizy said. "Unless you consider finding out if they've made some million-dollar bank deposits lately to be a reason."

We stopped for a red light and I glanced at Maizy. "Hey, how many rooms did you go into?"

"How many were there?" she asked.

"Three, not counting the living room and kitchen."

"Then three," she said.

I sighed. "Did you find anything other than a key?"

"Let me think." Carefully, she tucked the Play-Doh glob into her hoodie. "Ben-Gay, bran, bifocals, and No Flows. Lots of No Flows."

"Is that it?" I asked. "Think about it."

"Well, there was this." She whipped some papers from her hoodie.

"What is that?" Eunice asked. "That's a legal document."

"It's a power of attorney," Maizy said. "Abby was Oxnard's medical and financial power of attorney. Or at least she was."

"So what?" Eunice asked.

"So it means Oxnard trusted her enough to make life or death decisions for him." I thought about it. "I need to see

Oxnard's will. He asked Howard to draft a revised edition. I'd like to see what the changes were."

"That's easy," Maizy said. "You work with Howard. Just go look at it."

"It hasn't crossed my desk yet," I said. "And I don't want to scrounge around his office for it." Howard might bite me. I bit my lip, thinking. "She was furious about the idea of Sybil stealing her inheritance."

"Maybe that was her grief talking," Eunice said. "She's a poor old woman who lost her brother. I think it's tragic."

Maizy snorted. "You have a lot to learn about human nature."

"That's an awfully cynical perspective," Eunice told her.

"That's what happens when you ride the mean streets," Maizy said.

"I wouldn't know about that," Eunice said. "I'm from Montana."

"The thing is," I cut in, "I'm not sure I trust them. Alston remembered me. I didn't even speak to him at the wedding, and he remembered me. And I think Abigail was just pretending to be feeble-minded once he came into the room."

"So what are you saying?" Eunice asked. "You think that they killed their own brother?"

"That's what she's saying," Maizy told her. "Try to keep up."

"Only thing," I said, "why wouldn't they bump him off *before* he got married, not after?"

"What difference does it make?" Maizy asked. "He had a will, right?"

I nodded slowly, thinking. "But he did meet with Howard about revising it."

Eunice tapped me on the shoulder. "That's part of what I wanted to talk to you about. Howard asked me to draft the revised will, and I kind of lost his notes."

Oh, boy.

"The Thorpe will?" I asked.

She bit her lip. "I wanted to do it," she said. "I planned to do it. I just can't tell Howard."

And now Oxnard had gone and died, a newly married gazillionaire with an old outdated will, making who knew who the beneficiary.

"Don't worry," I told her. "Maybe the revisions weren't that important."

Her face lit up. "You think so?"

"Of course not," Maizy said. "You'll probably lose your job."

"She's not going to lose her job," I said. "Howard will understand."

"Sure he will," Maizy said. "Howard's a really understanding guy."

Eunice was toast.

I heard a giant sigh from the back seat. "I have to redeem myself," Eunice said. "Maybe we can find ourselves a nice five car pile-up on the way home."

"That's looking on the bright side," I told her.

* * *

"You want me to do what, now?"

He was a large man, with a barrel chest and a beer belly and a round, ruddy face and giant meaty hands that were presently holding Maizy's Play-Doh key impression. His name tag said *Sal*. His expression said *No way*.

"We need you to make a key," Maizy told him. She pointed. "Using that."

"Why do you need a key?" he asked.

"Because I can't walk through walls," she said.

I nudged her in the back. Because I was standing behind her. Because Sal was a little intimidating. Eunice was standing behind me, peeking over my shoulder, giving Sal a hopeful once-over.

"I mean," Maizy said, "I lost my key, and I need a replacement, and you have all those." She nodded toward the thousands of keys on display behind the counter.

"You lost your key," he said, "but you happened to have an impression of it?"

"You can't be too careful," she said.

Sal glanced past her to me. I looked away toward a very intriguing Roomba display. I liked the idea of a robot doing my cleaning for me. Then I saw the price tag and figured I could live with a little dirt.

"I got a daughter," Sal said.

"That's nice," Maizy told him. "So about that key."

"She's about your age," he said. "You're what, sixteen, seventeen?"

She got still.

"Last weekend," he said, "my daughter, she borrowed my car."

"Not sure where this is going," Maizy said.

"She didn't have a key to my car," he said.

"Technically speaking," Maizy said, "you don't always need a key. You can hot-wire a car in less than ninety seconds if you know what you're doing."

"She didn't hot-wire it," Sal said. "She had a key made, and she drove it away. And it's the last car she'll drive before she turns eighteen." He held up the Play-Doh, then brought his fist down on it and smashed it into a pink pancake. Then he handed it back to Maizy and walked away.

"Your logic is flawed," Maizy called after him. "That's not a car key." She shoved the pancake back in her pocket.

We looked at each other.

"You think he's married?" Eunice asked.

CHAPTER FIFTEEN

———

I spent the weekend in the usual way: sleeping and watching the Game Show Network and a *Munsters* marathon on TV Land. When I got home Monday night, I found papers wedged between the storm door and the frame. One was a bill from a florist for Sybil's white roses. A twisted part of me wondered if she'd recycled them as funeral flowers. The other was Lizette Larue's final invoice, with *Past Due, Please Remit* stamped in red on its face, underlined with a bright blue slash of marker. With a yellow exclamation point.

I had no idea who'd left them, or why they'd left them with me, but I dropped the papers on my kitchen table and put a mug of hot chocolate in the microwave. While I was waiting, Curt knocked on my door in faded jeans and a blue chambray shirt, untucked and open over a fire engine red T-shirt. "So you had a visitor pretty early Friday morning," he said when I answered it.

I gestured for him to follow me into the kitchen. "I hope we didn't wake you up."

"Nah," he said. "I got up early to watch the sun rise over the driveway."

I made a face at him. My level of maturity was a real source of pride.

He grinned. "I heard her climbing the stairs and knocking."

"Sorry about that. I wasn't expecting her. It was the new lawyer Howard hired."

"Yeah?" Curt leaned on the counter. "What's she like?"

"Her name is Eunice Kublinski," I said. "And I'm not sure. She seems a little unsure of herself." When she wasn't passing out business cards to old fogeys. And that driver waiting for AAA on the side of the road who hadn't believed she could sue her car manufacturer for a flat tire.

"Good trait for a lawyer," Curt said. "Got anything to drink?"

I opened the fridge. A moth flew out.

He sighed. "So how did it go with the zombies?"

I told him about Abigail and Alston and their lack of a real alibi. "Which suggested they maybe didn't go right home at all," I said. "But that they stuck around to kill Oxnard."

He was staring at me. "I'll pretend I didn't just hear that Maizy plundered the home of two senior citizens."

"That's not fair," I cut in. "She didn't *plunder* it. She just took advantage of Eunice being there to slip away and look around. Like she does."

"*Eunice* went with you?" he asked.

"We didn't plan it that way," I said.

"And yet," Curt said.

I sighed. "Are you going to stand there with your feelings hurt, or are you going to help me?"

"I can do both," he said.

"There's more." I told him about Bitsy's defunct business and shabby outdated home. "Why would she lie about something like that?"

"Embarrassment?" Curt said.

"Maybe." I thought about it, "It sure seems like Oxnard was a loyal friend, especially since they seemed to have so little in common as adults."

"They must have had something in common for her to be invited to the wedding," he said. "Unless he was just a sentimental fool."

I could give Oxnard the benefit of that doubt for the moment. "What about Abigail and Alston? They obviously lied to us."

"How do you know they lied?" Curt scrubbed his hand across his jaw. "Maybe Abigail thinks it's none of your business where they went."

I frowned. "I like my theory better."

"Okay," he said. "Let's go with that. Why?"

"She seems convinced Oxnard's house is theirs now," I said. "And probably everything else he owned. She thinks they're entitled to it. She called it *my house*."

"Wouldn't be the first time an estate got ugly," Curt said. "You should know that as well as anyone. After all, those two have been around forever. Compared to them, the bride dropped in two minutes ago. Did they have a good relationship with their brother?"

"According to Sybil, they saw him as their personal bank."

"But how did he see them?" Curt asked.

I thought about the so-called rehearsal luncheon. Sybil had claimed he'd wanted Abigail to be the maid of honor. But Alston hadn't been his best man. Interesting. "They don't think much of Sybil," I added. "They didn't come out and accuse her of killing him, but they stopped just short."

I opened the cupboard door nearest the fridge. A box of saltines and a jar of peanut butter. Good enough. I found a knife and got to work.

Curt took a saltine from the sleeve. "Did Sybil have a reason to want him dead?"

"She said he was having an affair. Maybe more than one."

"The miracle of pharmacology," Curt said.

I grinned.

"I'm thinking it wasn't a crime of passion," he said.

I agreed. I couldn't see it. Not that I tried too hard.

"There's another reason," I said, "but she didn't know it. Eunice was supposed to draft a new will for Oxnard, only she never got around to it." Although I couldn't imagine why. It wasn't like she'd had a full schedule and a desk full of work. Outside of meeting Penny Dollarz, she'd pretty much spent her days reading legal journals and cringing every time the phone rang.

"Let me make sure I've got this right," he said. "You have a greedy brother and sister and a new wife on one side with a groom who wanted to change his will on the other."

I nodded. "Sound like motive to you?"

"Could be," he said. "But whose?"

I spread some peanut butter on a few crackers and handed him one.

"Here's a thought," Curt said. "Maybe Sybil earned a payoff for marrying him in the first place."

I hadn't considered that. Had Oxnard bribed Sybil to marry him? Having met Sybil, I couldn't imagine why he'd want to, but my mother had always said there was someone for everyone. Of course, she'd been talking about me when she'd said it. My mother wanted nothing more than to see me married off, and she always said she planned to live until the day that happened, no matter how long it took. So clearly my mother was going to live forever.

But maybe Oxnard was an incurable romantic in search of a companion to hobble with him through the rest of his days. Only being Oxnard, he'd had to offer a fat payday to corral her. He'd have to offer *me* the Federal Reserve, but then Sybil could have planned all along to bump him off after the ceremony to collect her cash and find herself a human mate.

"I need to see that will," I said, thinking out loud.

"You mean the one that was never revised?" Curt asked. "Good luck with that."

I frowned at him. "What are you doing here, anyway?"

He smiled. "I'm glad you asked. I convinced Cam to order a little extra wall-to-wall."

"Is the man-cave ready for carpet already?" I asked, surprised.

Curt snorted. "It's not even ready for walls. Don't plan on seeing much of me for the next month."

I saw plenty of him. In my dreams. And when I peeked at him through the blinds every morning when he left for work.

He whipped a tape measure from his back pocket. "Anyway, I'm measuring for your new carpet. Any objections?"

"Maybe," I said. "Is it going to raise my rent?"

"I'm sure we could work out an arrangement."

I narrowed my eyes at him. "Would this arrangement involve someone getting naked?"

"Only if we do it right," he said. "We should probably practice. Follow me."

I followed him into the living room, thinking naked would probably be sexier than sweatpants, but I still wasn't ready to go there. I wasn't in a sexy place mentally. I didn't have the body for daylight seduction, and I didn't have the nerve for nighttime.

Then I took a look at Curt standing there showing off his dimples, in his faded jeans that hugged him in interesting places, his dark hair all mussed like he'd just gotten out of bed, and thought maybe I could wing it.

He pulled out a couple feet of tape measure. "Here. Hold this."

I forced my attention back to my sad Fruit of the Loom reality. "What?"

He grinned. "Take your dirty mind and go stand over there."

"I don't know where that's coming from," I said. "You have no idea what I'm thinking."

"Want to bet?"

Before I could react, he was in front of me, brushing my hair off my neck so lightly that I barely felt his fingers graze my skin, and then his fingers were replaced by his lips, soft and warm, planting little angel kisses below my ear. So he *did* have an idea what I'd been thinking.

Someone moaned, and I think it was me.

Curt drew back, smiling. "How'd I do?"

Like I was going to tell him, now that he was acting so smug.

"Not even close," I told him.

"I must be losing my touch." He let his index finger trail down my arm when he stepped away, a hint of a smile on his face when he retrieved his tape measure. "I'll try to do better next time."

If he did much better, my head would be on fire. I tried to gather my wits while I held the tape measure against the wall, watching while he got his measurements. "Aren't you going to write anything down?" I asked him.

"Nope." Curt motioned for me to let go and the tape measure withdrew into its casing. He dropped it back into his pocket. "So," he said. "You plan on eating peanut butter and crackers for dinner?"

"Have you got a better idea?"

He unleashed both dimples, almost making me drop my cracker. "I've got a lot of them, but let's start with dinner." He headed for my door. "Come on down in around twenty minutes." He winked at me. "Clothing optional."

Only if it was his.

CHAPTER SIXTEEN

———

Tuesday morning got off to a Monday sort of start. Phones rang constantly, clients tromped through with varying degrees of displeasure, and Eunice showed up in her finest shade of mud, clutching the Penny Dollarz file but looking no more comfortable with it. She headed upstairs without speaking. Donna crept up and down the stairs and in and out of the library without speaking, Janice stormed up and down the stairs and in and out of the client ledger files without speaking, Wally slithered in the back door and up to his office without speaking.

So things were starting to improve.

At eleven-thirty, I caught a glimpse of preppy out of the corner of my eye. An older version of Penny Dollarz stood at my desk. The same starched shirt, A-line navy skirt, and sensible pearl stud earrings. "Mora Dollarz to see Attorney Kublinski, please."

"Let me see if she's available," I said automatically. That was the standard line snatched from page one of the employee handbook, right next to *No sandals* and *Don't touch Janice's secret cookie stash.* I punched in Eunice's extension, which I belatedly remembered was Howard's extension until Eunice's new office was furnished.

"Yes?" he snapped in my ear.

"Mora Dollarz to see Attorney Kublinski," I said primly.

Eunice must have been sitting across from him. Howard said, "Mora Dollarz?" and then I heard Eunice say, "Oh dear," followed by a thump, a door slam, and another thump. Howard returned to the line. "I'm afraid she's unavailable at the moment."

I frowned. "That's not possible."

"It's entirely possible," he said. "Since she's lying unconscious on the floor."

"I'll be right there," I said.

Mora Dollarz had her arms crossed, her toe tapping, and her lips folded in on themselves like she was trying to seal in some dirty words.

"Attorney Kublinski may no longer be with us," I told her, which seemed true enough.

She uncrossed and unfolded herself. "We'll see about this," she said, jabbing a finger in my direction.

Like I never heard that before. In the meantime, I had to see about Eunice. I doused some paper towels with cold water and took the stairs two at a time. I found Eunice unconscious on Howard's sofa, her legs crossed at the ankles, her feet carefully angled off the leather. Howard knelt beside her, alternately fanning her with a manila file folder and slapping her cheeks.

He glared up at me. "What took you so long?" He snatched the wet paper towels and dropped them on Eunice's face.

"I had to get rid of Mora Dollarz," I said.

He pushed himself to his feet. "I'm not familiar with that name."

And he wasn't going to be if I had anything to do with it. I shook my head. "Maybe we should call 911. What happened?"

"Oh." He gave a dismissive little wave. "She heard you on the intercom and seemed quite anxious to see the client. In her haste, she tipped over her chair and ran right into the edge of the door, knocking herself out." He frowned down at her. "Maybe I shouldn't have moved her."

I didn't know about that, but I was pretty sure Eunice hadn't knocked herself out over eagerness to see anyone.

Wally flitted past the open door, stopped, backtracked, and stuck his head inside. "Everything alright in here?"

Howard said, "Of course" at the same time I said, "Absolutely not" and Wally came in. He paled when he saw Eunice. "Is she…"

"Passed out," I told him.

"Are you familiar with a Mora Dollarz?" Howard asked him.

I rolled my eyes. Note to self: don't ever require medical attention from a lawyer with a one-track mind.

"Dollarz. Dollarz." Wally gazed up at the ceiling, down at the floor, tapped his finger against his front teeth, ran a hand through his hair, crossed his arms, and said, "Never heard of her." He glanced at me, and his eyebrows twitched in the way eyebrows will twitch when trying to put the kibosh on honesty.

"How did this happen?" Wally stepped a half inch closer to get a better view, frowning down at Eunice as if he was peering over the edge of a very tall building.

Eunice's eyelids fluttered, she moaned once or twice, shook her head back and forth, and passed gas.

Wally stepped back. Howard turned his head with an expression of distaste.

Eunice unfolded her hands, seemed surprised to find herself lying on a sofa, patted herself down, seemed relieved to find herself fully clothed, and blinked up at everyone. "What happened?"

Wally and Howard retreated to Howard's desk, pretending to be engrossed in conversation. It was like watching two not particularly talented extras providing background activity on a movie set.

"Mrs. Dollarz wanted to see you," I whispered, and her eyeballs rolled back in her head a little. I put the paper towels back on her forehead. They flopped down over her eyes. She left them there. "She's gone now," I added. "I'm sure she just wanted to know how the case is going."

"It's not going so well," Eunice whispered. "To be honest, I'm a little lost."

"Emancipation cases aren't easy," I whispered back.

"It's not the case," she said. "It's me. To be honest…" She lifted a corner of the paper towel and one eye appeared, rolled over toward Howard's desk, and rolled back to me. "Maybe you haven't noticed, but I have a little problem with public speaking."

"You seemed fine with the Thorpes," I said. "You even gave them business cards."

"That was easy," she said. "I pretended I was handing out Halloween candy. It's different with actual clients."

"Penny Dollarz is only one client," I pointed out.

"It only takes one." She sighed. "Sometimes not even that. Sometimes it only takes the *picture* of one."

Geez. "But you're a lawyer," I said. "Didn't you do any mock trials before?"

The paper towel slid off her face when she shook her head. "Never." She swallowed. "Sometimes I practice in front of my mirror, talking to a picture of Chief Justice Roberts."

"That's a good idea," I said doubtfully.

"You'd think so. But see this?" She pointed to a yellowish bruised knot at the top of her forehead, beneath her hairline.

I nodded.

"Justice Kennedy," she said. "I hit the dresser that time. And this." She lifted her chin to show an inch-long scar. "The kitchen counter with Justice Sotomayor. And she's the *nice* one."

"Everything alright over there?" Howard boomed from across the room.

Eunice shot up off her back as if she was spring-loaded. "I'm fine, sir. Thank you for…" She hesitated, groping. "…whatever you did," she said finally.

Howard gave her a gracious Queen Elizabeth wave and turned his back on her.

I helped her to her feet. "Tell you what. You can practice on me. I'll be your jury."

Her face lit up. "Really?"

I nodded. I was pretty sure it was a better use of time than chasing down Oxnard Thorpe's killer. "You won't be arguing in front of the Supreme Court anytime soon anyway, right? When you get comfortable with me, maybe we can add someone else." I caught her panicked glance in Howard and Wally's direction. "Not them. Donna, maybe. Or Missy."

"I could talk to Missy," she agreed. "I think."

"Meet me in the conference room at five," I said. "You can give me part of an opening statement. Something short, say ten minutes' worth. Can you have something ready by then?"

"Sure, I have lots of opening statements," she said. "I've been passing out a long time." Her puppy dog eyes were moist when she gathered me into a hug. She smelled like Love's Baby Soft and her body felt like an oversized pillow. It was like hugging my grammy. I nestled into it and lingered there, wafting along on the gentle wings of nostalgia.

"This isn't a lovefest," Howard sniped. "Let's get back to work."

What a buzzkill.

CHAPTER SEVENTEEN

———

Three minutes into Eunice's bloodless mock summation, I was starting to wish *I* could pass out. After a few false starts and painful awkward lapses and one ill-advised scratching episode, it was pretty clear that she wasn't a born litigator.

But I'd spent my life rooting for the underdog, so I smiled at her and said, "Not bad. Now try practicing at home tonight using full sentences, and we can try again tomorrow."

She nodded. "Can I ask you something?" She struck an awkward pose, one hand on her hip, the other cupping an ear. "How do I look? Am I, you know…" She groped for the right word. "Lawyerly?"

Oh, boy. I had no interest in being mean, but the essence of Eunice was invisibility. Truth was, if Eunice was standing in front of a wall, you'd notice the wall first. All that brown and beige and *plain*.

"Yep," I said brightly. "You look just like a lawyer to me." I stood and grabbed my handbag. "That does it for me."

"Me, too." She smoothed the wrinkles in her skirt. "I think I'll head to the supermarket and see if anyone's slipped and fallen today."

There was hope for her yet.

I practically ran to my car and found Maizy waiting in the passenger seat, hood up, arms crossed, fingers tapping, and foot bobbing. She was the poster child for teenaged angst. "About time you got done," she said when I got behind the wheel. "Didn't you ever hear of a spare key?"

Sure I had. I'd also heard of revocation of license, spiraling insurance premiums, and multiple traffic infractions. That's why my spare key was tucked safely in my handbag.

I started the engine and backed out of the parking spot. "What happened to the Z?"

She studied her nails. Today's theme was spring green with tiny crystal daisies on the middle fingers. Nice. "It didn't stop."

Uh-oh. I glanced over at her. "What'd you hit?"

"*I* didn't hit anything," she said. "Except the brakes. The *car* hit Erving."

I stomped on the brake, and the Escort lurched to a stop halfway into the street. "You hit *Erving*?" Erving was half of Eugene and Erving, two monolithic police detectives who had shown up at the office to question me when Howard had been under suspicion of murder. The experience had been akin to talking to Mt. Rushmore, only with less satisfaction.

"He's fine," Maizy said. "I just grazed him. His 9 iron will never be the same, though."

I was having a hard time swallowing. "You mean he wasn't in a *car*?"

She rolled her eyes. "Of course not. You can't play golf in a car. It's not big enough."

Someone tapped a horn to our left. I backed up into the driveway again to let them and my heart palpitations pass. "Are you telling me you drove onto a *golf course*?"

"Once again," she said, "the *car* drove onto a golf course. That's the last time I believe it when Honest Aaron tells me he fixed a car. He's the worst mechanic ever. I could have been seriously hurt if someone had been practicing their drives."

I was pretty sure golf balls were the last thing she had to worry about. "You're lucky you weren't arrested," I told her.

"I'm a cop's kid," she said. "Who's gonna arrest me? I've got a bigger problem than that. Erving told me if he sees me driving again, he'll tell my dad. He had the Z impounded. Good thing there's no paperwork to tie it to Honest Aaron or I'd never get another car again."

"How about this." I let the car roll forward slowly again. "Why don't you forget about Honest Aaron."

She was studying her nails again. Her foot had quieted, and she'd pulled her lower lip back under the top one, where it belonged.

"You know, Maizy," I said, "My sister failed her test three times before she got her license."

"Your sister's a doofus," she said.

There was that. Speaking of my sister, I felt kind of bad that I'd never picked up that prescription. A week was an awfully long time to stand up.

"It doesn't make me nervous or anything," Maizy said. "Taking the test, I mean. If that's what you're thinking."

"I was wondering," I said. "Because you're so good at everything you do, it just seems strange that you keep inventing ways to fail."

"I don't invent them," she said. "They're just there."

I glanced at her. "You seem a little edgy today."

"I was thinking we should ask Dusty Rose about doing nicky-nack with Oxnard," she said. "Only I can't find her."

I heard the frustration in her voice. "What do you mean? Where did you look?"

"The usual places," she said.

Not too helpful, since Maizy's *usual places* could mean anything from the DMV to Department of Defense.

"Let's just say she's not in the usual databases," she added.

"Did you ask Sybil?"

She didn't say anything, but her bobbing foot picked up velocity. I took that as a no. Also as confirmation that you *can* be too smart. I'd always suspected it.

"We'll go to her house," I said.

Maizy brightened. "Cool. She did say she'd be happy to see us again."

That wasn't how I'd heard it.

"Can you drive a little faster?" Maizy jerked her thumb backwards. "That stuff is practically stale now."

I hadn't noticed the box in the back seat. It was full of food, but not quite food. It was a dollar store off-brand haul including bran flakes, a loaf of squashed white bread and a bottle of supplements for menopause symptoms.

Hm.

I looked at her. "Running away?"

"Get serious," she said. "I'd never eat that stuff. I bought it for someone. Since I don't have a car at the moment, Brody Amherst said he'll deliver it for me if he can have the vitamins." She snorted. "He could use the help."

Considering that none of Maizy's friends was menopausal, I had a feeling I knew whom the intended recipients were of her dollar store spree.

"That's really sweet, Maize," I told her.

"Yeah, whatever." She pulled her hoodie up. "The gas pedal's on the right, Grandma."

CHAPTER EIGHTEEN

———

"I'm glad you're here, Uncle Curt," Maizy said that night, on the way to Sybil's house. Maizy was driving Curt's Jeep. He was in the passenger seat. I was in the back, amusing myself by watching the wind ruffle Curt's hair. It didn't take much to amuse me.

Sybil's neighborhood was solidly lower upper class: not as ritzy as Oxnard's gated community, but far from Bitsy's tattered remnant of better days.

"I thought we might get stuck with Eunice again," Maizy added.

"What's wrong with Eunice?" I asked. Aside from fainting at pictures of Supreme Court Justices, that is. And her fear of public speaking. *Everyone* had a fear of public speaking. I'd read once that it ranked above death on the fear scale, which I could kind of understand. When you were dead, you didn't care much about humiliating yourself.

"She's not very brave," Maizy said. "I thought she was going to faint when Alston showed up."

Yeah, she kind of had.

"I thought she recovered pretty well," I said. "You just weren't there to see it."

"About that," Curt said.

"Huh." Maizy pointed. "Sybil's having a party."

We rolled to a stop at the curb and took a look. I'd expected the house to be less *Dark Shadows* than Oxnard's place, but not quite *Jersey Shore*, either. Every light in the house appeared to be on, and a thumping bass was rattling the windows. The sound of laughter and the intermittent clink of glasses drifted through the night air along with the smell of garlic and tomatoes and oregano, reminding me I hadn't had much for dinner.

It hardly seemed fair that I was out traipsing around the county in the dark while Sybil was whooping it up just days after Oxnard had groped his last. Clearly she wasn't worrying about who'd killed Oxnard. Because she already knew?

With Maizy and Curt behind me, I marched up to the front door and pounded on it. Instantly the music and laughter went silent. I glared through the frosted glass sidelight. No one in sight. "I know you're here!" I yelled. "Open the door!"

"No one home," a woman called out in a shaky voice.

I blinked. "Pandora?"

"Pandora's not here," Pandora yelled. "Go away!"

Fat chance. This had suddenly gotten interesting. I kept my finger on the doorbell until the door inched open and Pandora's eye appeared in the crack. "Oh, hello, Miss Jamie. You want to see Mrs. Sybil?"

I nodded. "Could you tell her we're here?"

Pandora's eye slid over in Maizy's direction, narrowing as she processed the blue hair, then widening as she processed Curt. Good luck with that. I'd known Curt for three years, and I hadn't been able to process him yet.

She pressed her cheek against the door, trying to block my view. "She isn't here. She hasn't been here for a few days."

"Of course she's here," I snapped. "I heard the noise. She's having a party."

"No, ma'am. You heard my brother Carlos and my cousin Luis and their girlfriends, Louisa and Angel, and Angel's sister Tori and—"

I was beginning to get the picture. The picture was an image of Sybil skulking around Oxnard's mansion, probably laying out plans for her new furniture and changing the locks on the in-laws.

"Can we come in anyway?" Maizy asked. "We need to ask you some questions."

"About what?" Pandora asked.

"We're detectives," Maizy said. "We're investigating."

"Well," I said, "we're not exactly detectives. More like…" I glanced at Curt.

"Nosy neighbors," he said.

I elbowed him in the ribs. He grinned and shrugged at me.

"I don't know..." Her eyebrow folded down and she glanced sideways and back to us. "I'm a little busy. Cleaning up the place, you know. For Mrs. Sybil."

"Don't worry," Curt said. "We won't say anything about the party."

She looked him up and down. He stood his ground, hands in his pockets, a small encouraging smile on his face, as unthreatening as a six-foot-two block of muscle can be showing up unexpectedly at the front door.

I decided to give her a nudge. "Pandora, I think Sybil might have killed Oxnard."

The half of her mouth I could see fell open. "Mr. Thorpe is dead?"

The door swung open, and five minutes later, we all had plates loaded with linguini and meatballs and some kind of delicious crispy bread and plates of roasted red peppers. It was like the rehearsal luncheon all over again, except this time with hospitality.

When Pandora sat down across from us, I noticed for the first time what she was wearing. Or more specifically, what she *wasn't* wearing. Her maid's uniform. I recognized her outfit as the one Sybil had worn to the office. She'd even borrowed Sybil's jewelry, judging by the emerald whoppers clipped to her ears.

I noticed something else. The drapes were lumpy and had feet. The dining room table, under its festive green tablecloth, had two pairs of hands. And unless I was off my game, the refrigerator was wearing a toupee.

Pandora and company had made themselves right at home.

"What happened to Mr. Thorpe?" she asked when she'd finally run out of things to serve.

Maizy was too busy snarfing her linguini to answer. Curt lifted an eyebrow at me.

"Sybil hasn't told you?" I asked her.

Pandora shook her head.

"Oxnard was found dead in the pool." No need to mention who'd done the finding.

She frowned. "I don't understand."

Maizy looked up from her plate. "The pool part or the dead part?"

"The pool part," Pandora said. "Why would he be in the pool? He was deathly afraid of the water."

"But..." I trailed off. Why would a man who was deathly afraid of water install a swimming pool? It was one of those unanswerables, along with why is the sky blue and what happened to my puberty.

Pandora glanced at me. "You said you thought Sybil had killed him. But if he fell in the pool and drowned..."

"We think he had some help falling," Maizy said.

"And the first suspect is always the spouse," I told her, with all the wisdom gleaned from my few inept homicide investigations.

"But there are always others," Maizy added. "So where'd you go after the wedding?"

Pandora gave a start. "I went home, of course. I had no reason to stay once..." She trailed off.

My ears pricked up. Once there was no one left to pay her? Once she'd killed Oxnard? Once she'd sampled the wedding cake?

Maizy had heard it, too. "Once what?"

"They paid me to cater the reception," Pandora said. "Not to clean up a pigsty after the fighting was done."

"What exactly went on at that wedding?" Curt asked me. "I thought you were kidding about that."

I did a *Tell you later* wave.

"Can anyone verify that you went home?" Maizy asked.

Pandora went a little pale. "I didn't go *straight* home. I went to the Dunkin Donuts and had some coffee and donuts."

"How long were you there?" I asked her.

She thought about it. "Probably nearly an hour. I needed to unwind, and I sat there reading the paper." She hesitated. "Am I a suspect or something?"

"We suspect everyone," Maizy told her. "It's what we do."

"Well, not *everyone*," I added. "That's a little bit of an exaggeration."

Pandora was shaking her head before I got the sentence out. "Don't be so sure, Miss Jamie. I heard Mr. Kantz and Mr. Thorpe arguing at the reception."

That must have been the argument before the food fight erupted.

"What were they fighting about?" I asked.

Pandora handed Curt a napkin. "I'm not sure. All I heard, Mr. Kantz told Mr. Thorpe to treat her right."

"Had Mr. Kantz ever been to the house to visit?" Curt asked.

Good question. I should've thought of it.

Pandora shrugged. "Not while I was there, but I went home after serving dinner. I'll tell you this—I wouldn't blame Mrs. Sybil for wanting someone else to talk to. Poor Mrs. Sybil." Her head lifted. "I mean Mr. Thorpe, of course."

Hm. That sounded like a clue. I put down my fork. "Pandora, did you like Oxnard Thorpe?"

She studied her shoes intently. "Certainly. He was good to Mrs. Sybil."

"Was he good to you?"

"Mrs. Sybil wanted me to stay on," she said. "And I needed the job."

Not quite the same thing. I felt the stirrings of suspicion. "Was he good to you?" I repeated.

Pandora shrugged. "Good enough."

I glanced at the drapes, the table, and the refrigerator. All feet, hands and hair were frozen in place. Probably everyone was eavesdropping as we discussed a subject that might be embarrassing to Pandora.

I eased back on the sofa. "Well, I didn't like him at all," I said loudly. From the corner of my eye, I caught Curt's small nod of approval.

Pandora's eyes widened. "You didn't?"

I shook my head. "He was always groping me. He's the reason I broke that vase, you know."

She grinned. "That was an ugly vase."

"Yes, it was." I smiled back. "He was a dirty old man, and I think she's better off without him."

Her smile faded. "He threatened to have me deported. I've been living in the U.S. for nine years. I made a good life here. And he threatened to report me to ICE."

"He did?" I stared at her. "Wait, are you—"

"I'm working on it," she said.

I wasn't sure where to go with that answer. It had never occurred to me that Pandora might not be in the country legally.

"Why did he do that?" Maizy asked.

She shrugged as if it didn't matter. "Mrs. Sybil talked him out of it."

I smelled a motive. But for whom, Sybil or Pandora?

"She said she wasn't about to go to the trouble of replacing me," Pandora added.

Charming.

"But why did he make that threat in the first place?" I asked quietly.

Her cheeks reddened. "He made many moves on me." Her voice dripped with disgust. "He thought because of my position, and his, that he could take advantage of me."

Something clicked into place, and it made deportation sound like the better choice. "Pandora, did he threaten to have you deported if you didn't sleep with him?"

Her lip curled. "I would *never,"* she said vehemently. "I'm a good Catholic girl. I would *never* do such a thing." She shook her head. "Are you alright? Can I get you anything?"

I was far from alright.

I suddenly had three more suspects.

CHAPTER NINETEEN

"Remember I was telling you about Ryan last week?" Missy asked me on Thursday morning. I'd spent over an hour immersed in the glamour of typing interrogatories in a product liability case for Wally. Interrogatories are a part of the discovery process, written questions that each party has to answer within a proscribed time period. They're multiple pages of pure tedium and one of the least favorite parts of my job.

"You were also telling me about Matt last week," I said. "It's hard to keep track." I sent the pages to the printer. Good riddance.

She shook her head. "Matt is so two weeks ago." She gazed at the ceiling with a small smile, lost in the nostalgia of Matt.

"Ryan?" I prompted her.

She blinked. "Oh. Right. You know what we did last night?"

I had a pretty good idea, but I pretended to listen anyway while I thought about Bitsy Dolman and the Stepford Thorpes and Pandora. All four had surprised me. Bitsy was a sad case, a woman who had apparently once been well off, but had fallen on hard times and into a bottle. I wondered if Oxnard had been aware of her situation, and why he would have remained in contact with her. Didn't seem like that would benefit his public image, but when you were King of the Adult Diapers, your image wasn't exactly gleaming to begin with. Maybe there had been more to Oxnard than met the eye. Maybe the two really had been friends for years, and he refused to turn his back on her just because her star had lost its twinkle.

Or maybe she was one of those obscenely rich people you read about who had millions stuffed in the mattress while living like a pauper. Hard to know unless she went on a sudden spending spree or a local cat suddenly inherited millions.

"So then he got some mashed carrots…" Missy was saying.

The Thorpes, on the other hand, hadn't waited long to dust off their sense of entitlement. They were an interesting pair. On the face of it, Alston seemed to be the one in control. He even looked the part. But beneath the surface, it was Abigail who wielded the power. And she definitely had a steely side. The problem was how to find out for sure where they'd been when Oxnard had been killed. I didn't know if I could.

And then there was pious Pandora, who'd hosted a kegger when Sybil had gone off for a few days and who seemed to have pretty good reason to want out from under Oxnard's wrinkled thumb. She knew her way around the Thorpe mansion, which gave her opportunity. She was under his constant threat of deportation, which gave her motive. And she could have easily gotten close enough to give him a good shove into the deep end before calling it a night. But had she?

"…and a pink tutu…" Missy said.

As far as motive went, I couldn't see any reason that Bitsy would want to kill Oxnard. She probably didn't stand to inherit anything. As far as I knew, they didn't have any business dealings together. And I just couldn't see it being a crime of passion.

Pandora had motive, and she had opportunity. But she almost certainly wouldn't benefit from Oxnard's will, and I couldn't see her killing him just for the thrill of it.

But Abigail Thorpe's motive slapped me in the face. She'd latched herself firmly to Oxnard's money, and he'd had the gall to go and get married, probably depriving her of it. I'd seen enough movies of the week to know that money was always a motive.

Which brought me to Sybil. She had the very same motive, plus a simmering side dish of revenge for Oxnard's diddling with Dusty Rose a possibility. Of course, she could have gone with the accidental death theory instead of agreeing to let Maizy and me investigate his death. Then again, maybe she was setting up a defense for what might be waiting down the road. Sybil struck me as cold and vengeful, but definitely not stupid.

And speaking of Dusty Rose, why would someone who looked like her diddle someone who looked like Oxnard? Unless...

I tried to recall my first conversation with Dusty in the kitchen at Oxnard's mansion. She'd mentioned her big break, and there'd been contracts on Oxnard's desk, but I couldn't remember the names on them.

"...and that's how Ryan and I discovered a new use for tube socks," Missy finished.

I stared at her. She gave me a small smile and turned back to her monitor.

All this not knowing left me with a whopper of a headache. It didn't improve when Eunice wandered downstairs as I was spell-checking Wally's complaint, encouraging the program to ignore such red flag words as "innards" and "entrails."

I noticed a big red welt on her forehead.

"Justice Ginsburg," she said when she caught me staring at it. "Are you busy? I have a summation I want to practice."

"Can it wait?" I asked. "I have to get through these files."

"Maybe I can help," she said. "I'm a pretty good typist, and it'll give me something to do."

"You're a lawyer," I told her. "Lawyers always have something to do."

She shrugged. "Not this one. Wally took the Dollarz file away from me."

I looked up from my monitor. "What? Why?"

Another shrug. "He didn't like my legal theory."

Neither did I, but geez, it was her first case, and Wally snatching it away seemed wrong.

"He must smell money," Missy said. "Is this the emancipation case?"

"Illegal imposition of curfew," Eunice said glumly.

"Maybe he'll give it back." I said. "Mora Dollarz doesn't seem too easy to deal with."

"I don't think so." She bit her lip. "I think I'm going to be fired."

"You haven't even been here a month," I said. "How could you get fired? You haven't done anything."

"That's the problem," she said. "Howard knows I didn't do that will."

And she hadn't been fired?

The phone rang. I held up a *wait a minute* finger and answered it.

"I've got an idea." Maizy. "Only we'll need some help. You're old, but not old enough."

I ignored that. I was usually three steps behind Maizy, but I had an idea where she was going this time. "No," I said. "We don't need an idea. We just have to go back to Oxnard's to talk to Sybil."

"She's not going anywhere," Maizy said. "She's got a pool and thousand thread count sheets."

"But I've got to see that contract again," I said. "I think it could be important. Dusty Rose could be a suspect, too."

"Of course she's a suspect," Maizy said. "They're *all* suspects. Your learning curve is kind of a straight line, isn't it?"

"What's your idea?" I snapped.

"You need to call in sick tomorrow," she said. "This is a daytime plan."

If I took many more sick days, Howard's next hire would be a staff nurse.

"We have to get to Herman Kantz," Maizy said. "Only I can't get an appointment with him. They keep telling me we have to deal with his minions."

"That's probably true," I said. "Anyone in an executive position has minions."

"I don't deal with minions," Maizy said. "We need to see *him*. So we need someone even older than you to pretend to be our grandmother."

"What good is that going to do?" I asked. "We'll still get foisted off on the minions."

"Sure we will," she said. "At first. But when Grammy starts talking about her millions, they'll be speed dialing Herman's extension."

I considered it. "Wouldn't it be better if Grammy says she's a childhood friend of Herman's and just asks to see him?"

Silence on the line. Then Maizy said, "Yeah, okay, maybe that'd work too. But we still need a Grammy. Unless you want to—"

"No," I said. "I don't."

Eunice whistled softly to get my attention and launched into a complicated series of gyrations.

"Hold on," I told Maizy. I looked at Eunice. "What?"

"You're detecting again, aren't you?" she asked. "Let me help. I want to help."

"Let her help," Maizy said in my ear. "She'd be a good Grammy. She's even got gray hair."

I tried to lower my voice. "She's not a grandmother."

"She doesn't have to actually *be* a grandmother," Maizy said. "She just has to *look* like one. And she does."

My eyes rose to the top of Eunice's head. Gray hair, check. Droopy eyelids, check. Saggy neck, check. Drab-colored old lady sweater, check. The Earth Shoes were just a bonus.

"You'd have to pretend to be a—" I began.

"Done!" Eunice's face lit up. "I can't believe I'm going to be detecting again. This is so cool!"

"Grammys don't use words like *cool*," Maizy said. "They use words like *delightful* and *educational* and *nutritious*."

"This is going to be none of those things," I told her.

"You don't know that," Maizy said. "This could be highly educational. Pick me up tomorrow morning." She hung up.

CHAPTER TWENTY

———

The offices of Kantz and Cochran were in a three-story building nestled into a leafy grotto along one of New Jersey's most picturesque highways. Unfortunately, the picturesque part didn't start for another thirty miles, leaving the tenants with unparalleled views of bumper-to-bumper traffic and a strip shopping center.

I found a parking spot in the rear, killed the engine, and we climbed out of the car. Eunice adjusted her bosom, which was now located several inches lower than it had been when she'd woken up.

"Are you ready for this?" I asked her.

She bit her lip. "Do *you* think I'm ready for this?"

"You'll be fine," Maizy told her. "Just smile a lot and say 'dearie' after every sentence. Oh. I almost forgot." She scrounged around in her backpack and came up with a skein of yellow yarn, a crochet needle, and a starter foot of scarf. "Hold this. Tell him you're making him a scarf. Old women are always making scarves."

"That is so not true," I said.

"Why are you doing this to me?" Eunice asked. "I didn't know I'd have to do all..." She gestured the length of her body. "...*this.*"

"What are you talking about?" Maizy said. "We're the ones who have to do the heavy lifting here. All you have to do is pretend you know this goober from a thousand years ago."

"But I *don't* know him." Eunice's expression was pure distress. "I don't think I can do this after all. I'm not cut out for a life of deceit."

"Of course you are," Maizy said. "You're a lawyer. Now listen up. Your name is Gertrude Moxley, and Herman gave you your first hickey."

Eunice's mouth dropped open.

I stuck my fists on my hips. "Seriously, Maizy? Why not go the extra mile and have him impregnate her?"

"An illegitimate baby?" Maizy stroked her chin, thinking. "That's a nice twist."

"We're not impregnating her!" I yelled.

Across the parking lot, a woman glanced our way and picked up her pace.

"I never had a hickey," Eunice said. She'd lost all the color in her face. Also, her left breast was about two inches higher than her right.

"You still haven't," Maizy told her. "It's called subterfuge. This guy is like granite. We need a way to get under his skin. Gertrude Moxley will get under his skin. She's done it before." She headed toward the entrance, tucking the blue hair under a baseball cap as she went.

Eunice grabbed my sleeve. "How does she know that?"

I gave her a palms-up shrug. Truth was, I didn't know how Maizy did half the things she did.

"That's not important," Maizy said over her shoulder. "You just get us into the inner sanctum and fade into the background, and we'll do the rest."

I was pretty sure Eunice had the fading into the background part down pat. She'd gone with her own wardrobe for the occasion: a ghastly floral-on-navy print dress that hung nearly to her ankles and was baggy enough to accommodate Maizy's vision of senior femininity: ugly tan support hose and a ginormous old lady brassiere armed with pendulous water balloons so heavy they hung to the vicinity of her belly button and made Eunice's shoulders hunch forward. Her wig was steel gray. She wore little steel-framed bifocals and orthopedic shoes. She could have been my Grandma Grace, if you ignored the fact that she sounded like a storm drain when she moved.

I'd never been to a financial planner's office because I had no finances, but I'd pictured the experience as something out of *Wall Street* with a lot of shouting and jostling set to the soundtrack of money changing hands. I'd been wrong. The walls were soft yellow, the décor was modern, and the floors were gleaming hardwood. The waiting room held a small television tuned to a muted CNBC. A dozen or so gray-haired clients were seated there, reading or watching the TV or napping. A lot of them napped. Most of them napped. I could barely hear the Muzak for all the snoring.

A perky twenty-something redhead was stationed behind the horseshoe shaped front desk. Her desk plate read *Deana*. Her expression was warm and welcoming. "Can I help you?"

Maizy and I nodded at Eunice. Eunice's face went stark white, and her eyes started to roll back in her head.

Deana made a move to stand. "Is she alright? Do you need a wheelchair?"

"She's fine," Maizy said. She reached out and pinched Eunice's arm hard.

"Ow!" Eunice's eyes rolled back into place, and she grabbed her arm. "*Res judicata!*" she yelled.

Deana glanced at me. "I'm sorry, what was that?"

"Grandma says things sometimes," I told her.

"*Ad vitam!*" Eunice agreed.

Deana's expression was slowly morphing into one of sympathy. She lowered her voice. "Are you interested in a financial Power of Attorney for your grandmother?"

"We're open to it," Maizy said. "But first she'd like to see Herman Kantz." She elbowed Eunice. "Wouldn't you, Grammy?"

"*Caveat emptor,*" Eunice said.

"Oh, I know that one," Deana said. She smiled at Eunice. "Were you a lawyer or something?"

"Lawyer," Eunice said. She slapped a business card on the counter.

"Isn't that nice," Deana said, reading it. "You still have some of your old cards." She hesitated. "This name sounds familiar. Isn't this the firm where that lawyer was killed?"

Eunice turned to me with an expression of pure horror.

I did a little head shake. "You must be thinking of someplace else," I said.

Deana shook her head. "No, I don't think so. It was Parker, Dennis and...someone else." She gnawed on her lip, thinking. A second later she snapped her fingers. "Heath! That's it. His name was Darren Heath. No, it wasn't." More gnawing. "Derek. No. Dabney?"

For God's sake. "Douglas," I snapped. "It was Douglas Heath."

"That's it!" Deana agreed. "Douglas Heath. He was murdered at the office. I read all about it."

"I quit," Eunice said.

Deana stared at her.

"Cute, right?" Maizy said. "She thinks she's still a lawyer. Sometimes we find her down at the courthouse in her briefs. She gets confused. So." She clapped her hands briskly. "You want to let Herman Kantz know Gertrude Moxley is here?"

"But..." Deana held up the business card. "This says Eunice Kublinski."

"That's her married name," Maizy said.

I rolled my eyes.

Maizy leaned forward on her elbows. "The thing is, this is kind of important to her. She's traveled a long way just to see Mr. Kantz again. They knew each other as kids."

Deana beamed at Eunice. "Isn't that sweet."

"Hickey," Eunice said.

Deana frowned. "What's that?"

"She said hickey," Maizy said. "He gave her her first hickey. It was a whopper. Her parents wouldn't let her out of the house for a month."

"Mr. *Kantz* gave her..." Deana's voice trailed off.

I glanced behind us. Still a few sleepers, but most of the clients had awoken and were tuned in to our conversation. One of the older men took off his glasses, cleaned them with his shirt hem, and stuck them back on to get a better look at Eunice. I couldn't blame him. She was bodacious.

"Chop chop," Maizy said, tapping on the counter. "Grammy's got to get to the salon. She's got a hot date tonight."

"Oh, I..." Deana's glance flickered to me. "I shouldn't...I really can't..."

Maizy turned to face our audience. "What do you mean, you don't want my Grammy's business?" she asked loudly. "She's just a little old lady who knits scarves. This is ageism!"

She gave Eunice a pointed glance, and Eunice thrust the yellow yarn into the air like she'd just won the Super Bowl.

"Hey," Deana said, "wait a minute. I never said that."

I leaned across the desk. "Grandma's got money."

"A *lot* of money," Maizy agreed. "Show her, Grammy."

Eunice hauled a rubber-banded roll of bills from her bag and waved it around. I was pretty sure it was a twenty wrapped around a bunch of ones. "*Quid pro quo!*" she shouted.

"She's rich now," Maizy said. "*And* she's got satellite TV."

The client with the glasses blew into his palm, sniffed it, and smiled at her.

Suddenly Deana was standing next to me. "Hold on, now. You can't come in here and disrupt the office like this. I'll have to ask you to leave."

Maizy pulled a box of Girl Scouts' Thin Mints from her backpack and held them up. "Anyone else want us to leave?" she yelled.

A lot of gray heads starting shaking.

"Anyone want a cookie?" she asked them.

The shaking morphed into nodding. Big smiles all the way around. Thin Mints were infinitely more exciting than anything that had happened with their investments lately.

"You can't do that!" Deana said, horrified.

"Lighten up," Maizy said. "Let them enjoy the two minutes they've got left."

"That's quite enough of that," a voice said behind us.

Maizy and I turned to find Herman Kantz glowering at us.

Eunice crashed to the floor in a dead faint.

CHAPTER TWENTY-ONE

"That was quite a performance out there," he said after we'd settled into his office. Maizy and I were in the client chairs. Eunice was sprawled on his sofa holding a bottle of Evian to her forehead.

The office was typical of that belonging to any late-middle-aged, overpaid, humorless autocrat. Heavy furniture, plush area rug defining a cozy seating area, walls the color of Bailey's Irish Cream dotted with photos of Herman with various local dignitaries. A golf ball on a tee in a little glass case sat on his desk, along with two legal pads, their edges precisely aligned, a gleaming silver ballpoint pen, oriented exactly one inch from the legal pads, a stack of mail at his left elbow, shuffled into an orderly pile one inch from the edge of his blotter. His blotter was one inch from the front edge of the desk. The phone was one inch from the top of the blotter.

I sensed a pattern.

"Hickey," Eunice moaned.

Herman Kantz ignored her. "Which one of you would like to tell me what that was all about?"

Maizy and I glanced at each other.

"You've heard about Oxnard Thorpe's death," I said.

He did a slight nod of assent.

"We're checking into it," I said. "We know you argued with him at the wedding. Can you tell us about that?" I was taking a chance in hoping that he didn't remember me sitting at the table alight in the glow of Sybil Sullivan's postnuptial charm, but it was a low risk chance. My life's experience had been that I was pretty forgettable.

Maizy gave me a *Well done* grin.

Eunice moaned softly.

"Don't tell me you three are police officers," Herman said.

Maizy shrugged. "Have it your way."

"We're detectives," I said quickly. "Private," I added.

"You don't look like detectives, either," he said.

"If we *looked* like detectives," Maizy said, "all those old people out there would think you're in trouble. They'd all be calling their lawyers to sue this place. See, we did you a favor."

"I can sue him," Eunice called. "*Locus delicti!*"

"If you wanted to talk to me," he said, "why didn't you just make an appointment? You didn't have to disturb my clients."

Sure, that was easy to say when we were already sitting in front of him, after sort of threatening a lawsuit, after creating a cookie frenzy, and after Eunice had wound up on the floor in a dead faint at his feet, her indefatigable bosom still in the unceasing ebb-and-flow of ocean waves.

"Who disturbed them?" Maizy asked. "They got Thin Mints. Everyone likes Thin Mints."

"So what did you argue about with Mr. Thorpe?" I repeated. I wasn't there to discuss cookies. Everyone knew Do-si-dos were the best.

"We didn't argue," Herman said. "We talked."

That's not the way I remembered it. I remembered the drink in the face that launched a food fight and ended in murder.

"Okay," I said. "What did you talk about?"

"I wished him well in his marriage," he said.

I lifted an eyebrow. "He didn't seem to take that well."

He did a slight shrug.

"What made him angry?" I asked.

"Business talk," he said. "A stock purchase, to be more specific."

That wasn't specific at all.

"Did you fight about No Flows stock?" Maizy asked. "It's down like 30% this week. They're going to have to sell a lot of diapers to make that up. And diapers cost a *lot* of money."

"I'm not at liberty to say," he said.

"It wasn't a question," Maizy said. "I *know* they cost a lot of money. My Uncle Odi wore diapers, only my Aunt Bea bought him Pampers 'cause they were cheaper than No Flows. They leaked a little, 'cause Pampers don't come in Ginormous Baby size, but she sewed two of them together and sent him off to watch football in his man cave all dry and happy."

I stared at her.

Herman stared at her.

Eunice lifted her head and stared at her.

"At least," Maizy said, "until he tried to change that light bulb and electrocuted himself 'cause he was standing in a puddle while he did it."

I cleared my throat. "Can you tell us where you went after you left the wedding?" I asked him.

He turned to me. "I went to the club. I had some dinner and took driving practice."

"What club would that be?" I asked.

He steepled his fingers. "Twining Valley Country Club. And that's not unusual. I often go there on Saturday nights. I've been a member for thirty years."

"Then I'm sure you ran into people you knew," I said levelly. "People who can confirm the time you got there."

Something flickered across his expression. Could have been annoyance. "I have nothing to hide. I got there at roughly quarter to ten."

I did some quick math. Wedding at nine, food fight at roughly nine-thirty, filet mignon at nine forty-five. I needed to find out how close Twining Valley was to Oxnard Thorpe's mansion. Then I needed to find out who could confirm his time of arrival.

"Had you been to the Thorpe home before?" Maizy asked him.

"Not that I recall," he said.

"Seriously?" Maizy said. "You never went over for caviar?"

Herman studied her for a moment. "Maybe once or twice," he said. "For dinner with Oxnard and Sybil."

"There you go," Maizy said. "Was that so hard? It's a nice place."

"I suppose," he said.

He *supposed*? Where'd he live, the Taj Mahal?

"They give you a tour?" she asked. "The kitchen, the pool, the hidden hallway?"

Oh, this was too much.

"I suppose," he said.

The guy was starting to really irritate me. Almost as much as being out of Maizy's loop.

Eunice had hauled herself off the sofa and was standing behind me, still clutching the skein of wool and listening raptly.

"Pretty smart," Maizy said. "You can go from the foyer to the backyard without even being seen. He had it built for access to his safe room, right?"

I'd assumed she'd done the usual self-tour: peeking in medicine chests and clothes closets and kitchen cupboards. I hadn't realized she'd drawn up floor plans. I'd have to have a long talk with her about her egregious invasions of privacy. And then have her design me a house.

Herman didn't answer her. But his lips had tightened, and his steepled fingers had collapsed and interwoven each other into one solid fist under his chin.

Maizy wasn't done. "Be a handy way to get from the pool to the naked David without being seen."

I heard Eunice whisper, "*Naked David*" to herself almost reverentially.

The phone did a little melodic *bleep* and Herman snatched it up. He listened for a few seconds, said "I'll be right there," and hung up.

"That was smooth," Maizy told him. "Deana called right at fifteen minutes. She's like a housebroken puppy."

"We're through here," Herman said, standing.

Eunice stabbed her finger in the air. "*Res ipsa loquitur!*"

"Get out," Herman said.

We got out.

CHAPTER TWENTY-TWO

————

"That was wonderful!" Eunice was beaming. "Wasn't I lawyerly? Except for the fainting part, I mean. I really think I can do this."

Her enthusiasm made me smile. "You didn't throw up or anything," I agreed.

She seemed surprised. "That's right, isn't it? I don't know what it is, but I feel comfortable with you two." She scooted forward on her seat. "Maybe I can help you out. You know, be your assistant. Since I don't have any files to work on right now."

"I don't think we need an assistant," I said.

"Give it some thought," Eunice said, warming to the idea. "I'm what you call an organizational thinker. Details are my thing."

"Let me think about it, okay?" I wasn't sure I wanted any more witnesses to my ineptness.

"You know where to find me," she said, satisfied for the moment as she looked out the window, humming gently.

"Speaking of details," I said to Maizy. "Didn't you forget to share a few?"

"Don't worry, I've got more," she said. "He's on a first name basis with SEC investigators."

"You don't want that," Eunice said. "That sounds like a big problem."

We rode in silence for a minute.

"Can we find out anything about Oxnard's financial situation? I asked.

"Sure," Maizy said. "There's no such thing as privacy anymore. What's on your mind?"

"Can we find out about that stock deal?"

"We can find out anything," Maizy said. "Except where Dusty Rose is."

"That's a pretty name," Eunice said. "I wish I had a name like that. It's hard being Eunice Kublinski."

"I feel you, sister," Maizy told her.

I rolled my eyes. "About that hidden hallway. You didn't mention any hidden hallway."

"Not important," she told me. "What's important is if Tiger Woods in there knew about it. He didn't seem too surprised when I mentioned it."

She was right about that. His granite expression hadn't changed a bit.

"The entrance is near the front door," she said. "Everyone would have thought he was leaving, except maybe he didn't. He admitted he was given a tour of the house. Maybe he sneaked into the hidden hallway and surprised Oxnard by the pool. Maybe Oxnard being near the pool was a happy coincidence."

Not for Oxnard.

"Except," I said, "why would Oxnard be near the pool if he can't swim?"

She shrugged. "Maybe Pandora was wrong."

"Then why would he drown?" I asked.

"Accidents happen," Maizy said. "Maybe he had a heart attack when Hermie was attacking him, and he shoved him in the pool. That would even *look* like an accident, right?"

"I guess," I said doubtfully. "But why wouldn't Oxnard yell for help if he was being attacked?"

"Because of the gun," Maizy said.

I blinked. "What gun?"

"The one Herman bought last year, right after he got his concealed carry permit," she said.

Oh, come on. "So you knew about his job and a hidden hallway and a permit and a gun," I said. "I'm starting to feel a little superfluous here, Maize."

"Not at all," she said. "You're the one with the car."

That made me feel much better.

"So according to his own timeline," I said, "it took him fifteen minutes to get from Oxnard's house to the country club. I think we should test that. We can start from the gatehouse; that's close enough."

"I'm all over it." Maizy stomped on the gas, and the Escort lurched forward, sucking wind like a vacuum cleaner and belching blue smoke out the rear.

Less than a half hour later, we reached Oxnard's gated community.

"If Herman killed Oxnard," I said, "I'm sure he was smart enough not to attract attention by speeding. Let's pretend to do the same. Does anyone know where Twining Valley is?"

"On Hidden Hollow Drive," Eunice said. "My brother used to caddie there when he was younger. I don't think Mr. Kantz killed anyone. He doesn't have the face for it."

"What does that mean?" I asked. "You can't kill someone with your face."

"That is so not true," Maizy said. "What about Medusa?"

"You had to use a mirror," Eunice said. "Then her face wouldn't kill you."

"So you have to walk around with a mirror all the time in case you run into a Gorgon?" Maizy demanded.

"Is that a problem?" Eunice asked. "Don't you powder your nose once in a while?"

"What for?" Maizy asked.

Eunice glanced at me.

I shrugged. "Five minutes gone," I said.

"The chef's name is Antoine," Maizy said.

"How could you possible know that?" Eunice asked her.

"I have contacts," Maizy said. "Plus I went to a little thing there a couple of months ago."
I looked at her. "You didn't tell me that."

"Not important," she said "And it'll never happen again."

"Was it a date?" I asked.

"Yes," Maizy said. "The sixth of February."

I rolled my eyes.

"Herman's favorite meal is boeuf bourguignon," she said.

"How could you possibly know that?" Eunice asked.

"Dude," Maizy said, "you have to stop saying that. No detective says that."

"She's right," I agreed. "A detective says *why* do you know that?"

Maizy shrugged. "The night was kind of a bust, so I decided to check out the kitchen. Turns out Antoine's a pretty chatty guy. He knows all the members through word association."

I nodded. "Like Brandon Broccoli?"

"Like Herman *Bouef Bourguignon*," Maizy said.

"Turn left at the next light," Eunice said. "Is Antoine married?"

"It didn't come up," Maizy said. "But he's like a giant, and he's got hair in his ears and a nose like a Koosh ball."

"I like tall guys who can cook," Eunice said.

Talk about looking on the bright side.

"Ten minutes," I said. "Are we close?"

"We're practically there," Eunice said. "It's just up around that curve."

Twenty minutes later, we pulled into the Twining Valley Country Club parking lot. Even that had the scent of old money, with its luxury cars and pricey landscaping.

"So a half hour," Maizy said. "Good call."

I watched a couple of men walk into the clubhouse. "So he couldn't have gotten here in fifteen minutes, but let's give him the benefit of the doubt and say he was wrong on that. Now the question is, did he come here at all?"

"Let's find out." Maizy got out of the car.

I got out of the car.

Eunice stayed put.

I leaned back inside. "Aren't you coming?"

She shook her head. "I think I'll sit this one out. I sprung a leak."

I grabbed some crumpled napkins from the glove box and passed them to her. She grabbed my wrist. "Take a picture of Antoine," she whispered.

I told her I would and followed Maizy around the back of the clubhouse and through the kitchen entrance into a raging beehive of activity.

We found Antoine in front of a huge six-burner stovetop working three pots and a sauce pan at the same time. He didn't seem too surprised to see Maizy. I got the feeling he'd seen her more than once before. And unfortunately, Maizy's physical description of him had been dead on. I pulled out my cell phone and took a quick picture for Eunice while he was busy devouring Maizy in a bear hug.

When he let her go, she rolled her shoulders around and moved her jaw back and forth, just to be sure. "We need to ask you something," Maizy said. "Was Herman Boeuf Bourguignon here on the night of the sixteenth?"

Antoine did some two-fisted stirring on the stovetop while he thought about it. Finally he shook his head. "Don't think so."

"Are you sure?" I asked. "Maybe he had something else for dinner."

"He never has something else," Antoine said. "Always Boeuf Bourguignon. And house red." He tapped his temple. "Antoine remembers." He hesitated. "Why?"

"We're solving a murder," she told him.

His jaw went slack. "HBB was killed?"

"HBB's client was killed," Maizy said. "Oxnard Thorpe."

Recognition flickered across his face. "Oxnard Pasta Primavera is dead?"

"Guess so," Maizy said.

Antoine's lower lip began to tremble. "But he was such a nice old guy. When he sold the business last summer, he started living it up, coming in a couple times a week. Always ordered white truffles, and tipped a hundred dollars if we brought it to him poolside."

My ears perked up. "A hundred dollars?"

Maizy rolled her eyes. "Sold the business?" she asked.

Antoine nodded. "Told Gil he was happy to see it go. I don't blame him. Pay me a few mil and I'd be happy to spend my afternoons poolside, too."

"Poolside?" I repeated.

Another nod. "OPP didn't golf. He came in to use the pool."

"Like sit on the edge with his feet in the water, right?" Maizy asked.

"Wrong," Antoine said. "Like leering at all the pretty women from a deck chair."

That seemed about right for Oxnard.

And *Eww*.

"Did you ever see him swimming?" I asked.

Antoine frowned. "Well, no. I never saw him at all. Gil would take the truffles out to him, and he'd always say OPP had his eye on someone or other at the pool."

"Is Gil here?" Maizy asked.

He shook his head. "Haven't seen him. He must be off today. I can ask him about OPP and call you tomorrow, if you want."

"Thanks, Tony." Maizy executed a standing high jump to plant a peck on his chin. "Catch you later."

I grabbed her arm as we headed back to the car. "You said you were only here once."

"No, I didn't," she said. "That's what you *heard*. See how it works?"

That wasn't an argument I could win.

"Do you think Pandora lied to us?" I asked.

"Everyone lies to us," Maizy said. "That's where the detecting comes in."

Eunice was napping in the back seat when we got back in the car. A big water stain darkened the left side of her chest, and it wasn't from her drooling.

"What are truffles, anyway?" I asked Maizy.

"Fungus," she said. "Expensive fungus. Especially white truffles. Very rare."

"How could you possibly know that?" Eunice had woken up.

"Now you're just embarrassing yourself," Maizy told her.

Eunice tapped my shoulder. "Did you get it?"

I passed my cell phone back to her. I heard a gasp, and then Eunice said, "The man is a *god*. Do you think you can introduce me?"

CHAPTER TWENTY-THREE

———

I dropped off Eunice at her car and Maizy at her house and stopped at the supermarket to pick up nice, healthy frozen pizza slices for dinner along with a few necessities: Chips Ahoy, Butterscotch Krimpets, and a quart of French vanilla ice cream. I switched on the TV, fixed Ashley's dinner, slid the pizza in the oven, stashed everything else in its appropriate place, and headed straight for the shower.

I stood under the hot spray for as long as I could take it, rotating a few times for balance, and then climbed into my most worn sweatpants and sweatshirt and settled in with the pizza. The TV was showing an ancient black and white game show where a glamorous panel tried to guess the contestant's occupation. It was a diabolical premise because people were never what they seemed. But they did their best with it while I finished off the slices and moved on to doing ten minutes of triangle and warrior poses before settling into shavasana, allowing my entire body to melt into complete relaxation.

Except my body didn't want to relax. And my mind didn't want to stop spinning. After ten minutes, I decided yoga wasn't going to do it and found myself downstairs at Curt's door.

He answered the door in jeans, bare feet, no shirt, with a bottle of beer in his hand. We went into his living room, where *Die Hard* was on the TV. Alan Rickman and his henchmen were just crashing the party at Nakatomi Plaza.

"You know what I never got about this movie?" I asked, accepting the bottled water he offered. "Who takes off their shoes and socks in a public bathroom?"

"*That's* what you never got?" Curt dropped onto the sofa beside me. "Clearly you don't appreciate excellence in cinema."

I watched Hans Gruber with his perfect hair and immaculate suit and thought maybe I should work on that.

When the action moved to the conference room with Mr. Takagi, Curt lowered the volume and said, "So who killed Oxnard Thorpe?"

Which was the opening I needed. I put down the water bottle and told him about Herman and his problems, and Abigail and Alston's rampant entitlement, and Bitsy's eagerness to implicate Sybil, and the visit to Herman Kantz, and our conversation with the new love of Eunice's life. As usual, Curt listened without commenting, his attention fully on me.

"And you already know he threatened to have Pandora deported," I said. "Or so she says."

He nodded. "What's your impression of the brother and sister?"

"I'm not sure," I said. "I don't trust Abigail, and I get a coldness from Alston, but I think they genuinely loved their brother. I mean, they tried to defend him at the reception."

"Maybe big Al had a thing for Sybil and wanted his brother out of the way."

I gave him a look.

He shrugged. "Heat of the moment?"

Passion and heat weren't the two things that came to mind when I thought about Oxnard's family, but you never knew. Arguments happened, just like accidents did. Maybe they hadn't meant to shove Oxnard into the pool. Maybe they'd just pushed him a little, and he'd lost his balance. Or maybe Herman had held a gun on Oxnard, and he'd had the heart attack Maizy suggested and tumbled into the pool himself, saving Herman a bullet. And probably me as well, since I'd been just on the other side of the solarium glass at the time. A shiver ran through me.

"The problem is," I said, "I don't know who actually left the reception and who just pretended to leave. The place is huge, and there's a hidden hallway that runs the length of it."

"Sounds like something his family would be aware of," Curt said.

I nodded. "Probably Pandora, too. And Sybil for sure. Even Herman admitted knowing about it."

On the TV, John McClane was making his barefoot escape from the restroom to the upper floors of Nakatomi Plaza.

"How's this," I said. "Maybe Alston and Abigail planned to stay the night rather than drive home. And they fought with Oxnard about Sybil after she left. Things got out of hand, and he fell in the pool by accident, and they panicked and ran off." Well, maybe *ran* wasn't the right word. Shuffled. In tandem.

Curt went to the kitchen and came back with another beer and a bag of pretzels. "Or," he said, "Sybil shoved Oxnard into the pool herself after catching him with that girl he cheated with."

"Dusty Rose," I muttered. I shook my head. "Dusty's gorgeous, but I don't see it. Not with Oxnard." Although we hadn't tracked her down yet, either, so I could only wonder about her alibi.

"You don't know her," Curt pointed out. "You don't know any of them."

Something occurred to me. "You know, Oxnard recently met with Howard to discuss changing his will."

Curt frowned. "Did Sybil know about that? She might have had reason to accelerate his death if she stood to inherit millions."

"She knew," I said. "She came into the office with him. But she wasn't there when he met with Howard. She'd stayed downstairs, with me."

"We can assume he put his wife in his will," Curt said. "Why don't you take a look at it?"

My mouth twisted. "I can't find it. No one's asked me to type it. And Eunice lost Howard's notes. So there's no way of knowing what changes he was making."

On the TV, John McClane scurried barefoot around the upper floors of Nakatomi Plaza.

"There is another possibility," Curt said. "Could be we're completely wrong and it'll turn out to be a break-in gone bad."

"It's a gated community," I said.

"Gated communities are only as good as the security," Curt said.

The idea didn't feel right to me. A stranger wouldn't have known the house well enough to get in and out and kill the homeowner in between without being heard or seen by people left behind. Namely, Maizy and me. And a stranger wouldn't have known that Oxnard couldn't swim. That knowledge would be confined to family or friends.

Besides, we had enough suspects just from the wedding. We didn't need to add a homicidal burglar to the mix. Bad enough we had a homicidal wedding guest.

CHAPTER TWENTY-FOUR

———

On Monday morning, I almost didn't mind that Eunice's Legume was parked in my space. I parked beside it, crossed the lot under a warm late spring sun, and opened the back door.

I was immediately trampled by a fifty-something couple, the woman being propelled with a firm fist to the lower back by her grim-faced husband. Followed by Eunice, calling "Mr. and Mrs. Wilfork, please reconsider!" She flapped several legal-sized pages at their backs, but that only pushed them faster toward the black Mercedes parked in the spot nearest the door. Howard's spot. Mercifully, Howard wasn't in yet to witness whatever this was. With any luck, Wally wasn't, either.

I stepped in between Eunice and the Wilforks and shut the door firmly, letting the couple escape. "Do we need to discuss?"

Eunice drew up short, her shoulders drooping. "I thought I'd talked them into it."

If *it* was a hasty exit and an ethics complaint, she may have. I steered her away from the door.

She slumped across the room while I booted up my computer. "I don't understand it," she said glumly. "They have the perfect case. They just didn't understand my concept."

I stowed my handbag in the bottom drawer. "Which was what?"

Her face brightened. "Discrimination."

Finally, valid grounds for a lawsuit. I recalled Doug Heath had once sued a strip club on the grounds that it hired only dancers of generous frontal proportion, thus discriminating against lesser endowed girls. He'd hoped to make it a class action suit, but couldn't find enough plaintiffs, even though he'd scoured every strip club in New Jersey in a diligent search. "Was he applying for a job?" I asked.

Eunice blinked. "How would I know? I met them at the supermarket. Arguing." She cleared her throat. "In the condom aisle."

Oh. Oh, my.

"It seems they didn't carry his...um...size."

"They come in sizes?" I asked.

She blushed furiously. "I guess so. I was only passing through, not, um...shopping. I was on my way to the heat patches. You know, because I've had a lot of falls lately." She flashed me her bruised forearm as proof.

"The Supremes," I said with a nod.

She gave me a wan smile. "So we got to talking, and Don—that's his name, Don—he said it wasn't right that females can get training bras but males can't get...well..." Her cheeks flushed.

I'd had it all wrong. I felt a stab of sympathy for Don.

"Anyway," Eunice said, "I told him I thought he was right. And I advised him to come see me. As a lawyer. I mean, he can't be the only one, can he?"

"I wouldn't think so."

She nodded. "It's a classic case of size discrimination. And we can throw Patrice—that's her name, Patrice—in for loss of consortium."

"Eunice," I began, but I had no idea what to say to her. Maybe I should offer to help with her résumé.

"It's got class action written all over it," she said. "Only how would I go about finding all the other Dons?"

"I can't imagine," I said. My voice sounded faint. Wait till Wally got wind of this.

"Maybe a television commercial." She put down her papers and rolled her eyes up to the ceiling, pondering. "Everyone watches television, right? We word it just the right way, this place will be swimming with clients. The key is not to embarrass them. We have to make like it's no worse than bad breath or dandruff. So they're willing to testify in court. And pose for photographs. I'll get right on it." She smiled. "You know, lawyers get some pretty good stories. Maybe I'll write a book."

I looked up in alarm. "You can't write a book! You'll violate attorney/client privilege!"

"Oh, yeah. There's that, isn't there." She chewed on her lip, thinking. "Maybe I'll wait till I retire. I'll need to make money somehow. It's not like my giant pension will carry me through my golden years. Hey." Her face brightened. "Do you have to go interrogate anyone?"

I nodded. "But it's sort of a do-it-yourself kind of job."

"Oh." Her shoulders dropped even more. "Well, I guess I'll go hide in the conference room, then."

"There's a deposition starting at ten," I told her.

She shrugged dispiritedly. "No one will notice me. I'll just blend into the woodwork."

Not true. The woodwork had some style to it.

CHAPTER TWENTY-FIVE

———

I had a lot of thinking to do, but I wasn't going to get it done on Howard's time. The morning began with a flurry of activity and devolved into a blizzard. Five attorneys and their respective clients, together with a court reporter, each with different beverage requests, were tucking into the conference room with Howard and Wally for the lengthy deposition of a defense expert. Eunice had been evicted from the conference room and told to make herself useful, which she did by taking a vacation day. Janice was rushing around juggling luxury car brochures. Donna was rushing around collecting books from the library and squirreling them away upstairs for some obscure project or other. Ken didn't rush anywhere—he strolled in at about ten-thirty and went upstairs for his morning nap. And Missy had been happily dispatched to the nearest bakery to acquire sufficient amounts of sugar to keep all parties alert until quitting time.

The end result was an unusual level of productivity, but a vague sense of restlessness to go along with it. Mostly because I wasn't doing so well in sniffing out Oxnard Thorpe's murderer.

That unhappy thought carried me until nearly five o'clock, when it hit me that there was actually something I could do. I clicked onto the Web, where I typed "Fire and Ice show" into Google. For some reason, I couldn't reconcile Bitsy Dolman with fashion shows, which of course didn't mean she'd knocked off Oxnard Thorpe. Still, it seemed somehow important to confirm her attendance at the show, since it was, after all, her alibi.

I clicked on the link to the official Fire and Ice website. An impressive slide show of untouchable models in unwearable couture appeared on the screen. Lots of bare skin and ludicrous feathery headwear and see-through gowns. I really didn't get fashion.

There were a series of buttons across the top of the page. I clicked on the one that promised a history of the celebration of philanthropy that was Fire and Ice. It was standard PR fare: the designers participating in the show represented the vanguard of the fashion industry, blah, blah, blah. And a little further down, what an honor it was to be in Chicago for this year's annual show.

Chicago? How could Bitsy have possibly attended Oxnard's wedding and been in Chicago for a fashion show on the same day?

She couldn't. Even if the flight schedule worked out, which never happened, Bitsy wasn't in the financial position to play jet-setter. Or to celebrate philanthropy. Which meant she'd lied. The question was why she'd felt compelled to lie to *me*. That was one I'd have to think about, preferably over a container of fast food chili.

I closed the browser, shut down my computer, and headed for my car when Eunice's Legume came rocketing into the lot and screeched to a stop in front of me. "Get in."

I kept walking. "I'm off the clock."

The Legume crept forward, keeping pace. "But I have information about the case."

"Eunice." I stopped with a heavy sigh. "You can't sue a condom manufacturer for not making a pee-wee size. Or file an improper imposition of curfew suit. I don't know where you went to law school—"

"Harvard Academy of Law," she said helpfully. "And Mortuary Science. Online."

Right. "I'm going to get some chili and go home." I started walking again.

"Got it." She inched the Legume ahead. "But that's not the case I'm talking about. I mean the murder you and Maizy are investigating."

Investigating. Good one. Maizy could probably find Amelia Earhart. All *I'd* done so far was gotten lucky with a simple internet search.

Then it hit me, and I stopped again. "What are you talking about?"

She grinned up at me. "I went back to see those old people again today."

Oh, no. "You don't mean the Thorpes."

The office door slammed, and Janice stomped across the lot, lugging a bulging leather portfolio. She saw us, looked pointedly at her car beyond Eunice's, and said, "Move."

The Legume immediately backed into a spot, maybe of its own volition. I sauntered after it, moving at an arthritic elephant's pace to sour Janice's sunny mood.

"Do you mean the Thorpes?" I asked her when I finally got there.

"Yeah, I do. The Thorpes." Her grin widened. "About the probate of Oxnard's will. Remember, they were waiting for the paperwork?"

"You don't have any paperwork," I said.

She did a dismissive wave. "Are you kidding? This place is nothing *but* paperwork."

I stared at her. "Are you telling me you took papers out of other files?"

"Only one file. And just a few papers." She shrugged. "They never knew the difference. They saw a briefcase, some documents, and a lawyer, and they think they've got a fortune coming to them."

"Maybe they *do* have a fortune coming to them."

She waggled a single finger. "Murderers don't get to profit from their crime. And those two killed their brother. Well, maybe not both of them. But one of them did, and the other one's covering for him—or her—and that makes him—or her—an accessory."

I felt a headache begin to gnaw at my temples. "How do you know that?"

"I'm a lawyer," she said cheerfully.

Janice roared out of the parking lot. She may or may not have flipped us the bird along the way—I wasn't paying attention. I was busy watching Donna creep out the back door. She did a finger waggle wave, tucked herself into her car, and putted off, leaving Eunice and me alone again.

"What I mean," I said patiently, "is how do you know they killed their brother?"

"After we went over the paperwork," she said, "we drank tea. And ate sponge cake." Her grin faltered. "I shouldn't have eaten the sponge cake. I'm kind of on a diet."

I wasn't connecting the dots. "I don't get it," I said.

Eunice tapped impatiently on the steering wheel. Her fingernails were short and unpainted, with a few ragged cuticles. "They told me they're Oxnard's sole beneficiaries. You know, in his will. That means—"

"I know what it means," I said. "How do they know that?"

"Abby said Oxnard told her," Eunice said. "When he had it drawn up."

"Did she see a copy?"

Eunice shook her head. "She said he filed it in his office."

"Did Howard draft the original?"

"I didn't ask." She seemed crestfallen. "Should I have asked?"

It probably didn't matter. The will was the will, regardless of who had drafted it. And if Abby and Alston thought they stood to inherit Oxnard's estate, that gave them millions of reasons to want to expedite the process. I remembered the scene at the pharmacy. It seemed they could use the money. And it was clear they coveted the mansion.

I smelled motive.

I hurried around her car and climbed into the passenger seat. "You did a good job, Eunice," I told her. "I'm taking you out for a nice dinner."

She laughed. She had a nice laugh. She should work it into her courtroom repertoire, if she ever saw the inside of a courtroom. "I did? Where are we going?"

I did a quick assessment of my finances. "Wendy's."

"Works for me," she said.

CHAPTER TWENTY-SIX

―――――

"It's not my fault," Maizy told me over Tuesday night dinner in my apartment. Ashley snored gently in her lap. Gene Rayburn orchestrated *Match Game* on the Game Show Network. Empty cartons of Chinese food littered my coffee table while I cracked open all the fortune cookies in search of a brighter future. No luck so far. The early evening sun slashed through the blinds, striping the floor in skinny golden bars.

A big brown shopping bag sat four feet away from me on the floor. I didn't like the looks of that bag.

Keep an open mind.

"None of this would be necessary if she had agreed to talk to us," Maizy grumbled. "I only asked her one question, and she hung up on me."

She was Sybil Sullivan Thorpe, who hadn't been very wise when she'd done that about three hours earlier. Obviously she didn't know that Maizy refused to be dismissed and would not be thwarted.

"She's hiding something," Maizy said, stroking Ashley's fur slowly. "I know it. I could hear it in her voice."

Be more open to adventure.

I sneaked another peek at that bag.

"So I thought we should go talk to her," Maizy said. "Only she's squatting at Oxnard's house. I checked. We have to get back there."

"How do we get past the gatehouse?" I said. "Hike through the woods and climb over the fence?"

"We drive in like everybody else."

I cracked another fortune cookie. *Test your boundaries.* I was getting tired of getting life coaching from a cookie. I shoved the rest away.

"What are we supposed to drive in?" I asked. "The Escort? The Z?"

She pointed. "The Bentley."

"*What?*" I leaped up and ran to the window. A shiny tan Bentley sat in the driveway, so fancy that I could practically see dollar signs floating in the air above it like champagne bubbles. I spun around. "Where did you get a Bentley?"

She shrugged. "Where does anyone get a Bentley? It's Honest Aaron's."

My jaw dropped. "You're kidding me. He rents out those dumpster fires on wheels, and *he* drives a Bentley?" I took another look at it. It practically twinkled. "How much?" I asked.

"No charge," Maizy said. "On account of I'm in the Gold Plan. Also, turns out I know his girlfriend. She's in my English class."

Eww. "He ought to be in jail," I said, outraged.

"Why?" Maizy asked. "She's 23. Tami's kind of a dangling participle, if you ask me. Anyway, the car has to be back tonight. She wants to use it tomorrow. And Honest Aaron needs to pick up his wife at the airport tomorrow night."

Life just wasn't fair.

"There's just one thing," Maizy added.

Here it came. I glanced at the bag, pretty sure that was the *one thing*.

"We still need a way to get in," Maizy said. She pointed. "And there it is."

"I don't like it," I said. Which was kind of a reflex when it came to Maizy and her schemes.

"You don't know," she said. "Give it a shot. Old people never remember how to have fun. *God.*"

Well, I wasn't going to stand for *that*. Not until I hit 35, anyway.

"Give me the bag," I snapped. "I'll show you how to have fun."

Ten minutes later, I stepped out of the bathroom in the world's worst fitting chauffeur uniform. The pants drooped badly and dragged on the floor, the jacket hung to mid-thigh, and the only thing keeping the cap on my head were my eyelashes. I was *Big* meets *Driving Miss Daisy*.

And I was so *not* having fun.

Maizy hadn't changed a bit in the time I'd been gone. Frayed jeans, Doc Martens, black midriff shirt that showed off a sparkling blue belly button ring, smudgy black eyeliner and hair in a full blue poof. The black hoodie had been left behind, providing a cozy bed for Ashley, who was kneading it furiously in preparation for her pre-bedtime nap.

I tried to set my cap farther back on my head without success. The thing had been made for a candy apple head. "What are you supposed to be?"

She blinked at me. "I'm Oxnard's free spirited granddaughter Willow."

"Doesn't seem too free spirited to have a chauffeur drive you around in a Bentley," I muttered.

"Would it be more believable if we drove up in your car?" she asked.

Good point.

She headed for the door. "Now pull up your pants and let's go get some answers."

*   *   *

The Bentley was everything I'd hoped it would be. Substantial and light at the same time, *whishing* over bumps and potholes like the whisper of silk over bare skin, gliding down the road with the grace of a majestic eagle soaring through the wilderness.

It was a flight on the wings of automotive fantasy except for one thing. The steering wheel was on the wrong side of the car. I almost took out two stop signs, one fire hydrant, a picket fence, and a Volkswagen Beetle before we dropped anchor a half hour later. The guard was snoring in his gatehouse, a copy of the *National Enquirer* splayed open across his chest and his feet propped up on the counter.

I tapped the horn as gently as I could. Its blast shattered the silence like the horn of a cruise ship. Possible that Honest Aaron had done a little tweaking there.

The guard's feet fell off the counter, his cap fell off his head, and the *Enquirer* fell off his chest all at the same time. His window slid open and he stuck his head out, looking at us a little wildly. "Wha...?"

"Oxnard Thorpe's granddaughter is here," I told him. "If you'll buzz us through."

He nodded energetically. "Of course. I..." He hesitated. "But why? The place is empty."

Interesting. He didn't know Sybil was there.

"Is there a problem?" Maizy called from the cushy acreage of the back seat. "Willow won't be happy if there's a problem."

The guard leaned toward me and whispered, "Who's Willow?"

I pushed my cap out of my eyes and pointed my thumb to the back. "She is."

He glanced at Maizy. She flashed him a peace sign.

He scratched his forehead. "I gotta be honest," he told me, "I didn't think Mr. Thorpe had any kids."

The back window slid down and Maizy held out a fifty-dollar bill. "Is that relevant?" she asked.

The fifty disappeared into his pocket. "Not to me," he said.

Five seconds later, the gate swung open with excruciating slowness, and I navigated the Bentley through the exclusive community as though in a Fourth of July parade, not exceeding five miles an hour and staying as close to the center of the street as possible to avoid clipping a curb or a thousand-dollar hedge.

David was once again a monument to incontinence when we parked in Oxnard's circular driveway. Good thing Oxnard had manufactured adult diapers instead of erectile dysfunction medication. Other than David's immodesty, the house was ready for a magazine layout. The lawn was perfect, the flowers in riotous bloom, the hedges trimmed. The Bentley was right at home.

I peeled off the ridiculous chauffeur outfit and left it in a heap on the front seat, pretty sure it had been solely for Maizy's entertainment anyway.

Sybil opened the door on the third knock, dressed in black. No red eyes. Full makeup. Her hair was done in one of those slicked-back low ponytails that looked simple but probably took a half hour to accomplish. "What do you two want?" she demanded. "How did you get in here?"

"You hung up on me," Maizy said. She brushed past her into the house. While Sybil was busy staring after her, I slipped in behind her, clutching the two invoices.

"These were left at my apartment," I told her.

"I have no time for this," she snapped. "I have things to do."

Odd. I thought vampires did their best work after dark.

"We won't take long," Maizy told her. "We have some questions."

"Such as?" Sybil's fists went to her hips.

"Such as," I said, "did you know Oxnard sold No Flows a year ago?"

Her face slackened. "That's ridiculous. He would have told me."

"Would you have married him if he did?"

Sybil hesitated for a beat. "Of course. I loved him."

My gaze went to her bare ring finger.

"How about if he made Abby his sole beneficiary?" I asked.

Sybil's lips tightened into a white slash. "Nonsense. I was his sole beneficiary. He told me so. What are you trying to pull?"

"We're just trying to figure out who killed your husband," I told her.

"Well, I certainly didn't do it," she snapped. "Why would I marry the man if I intended to kill him?"

To guarantee her inheritance?

"If you two are done," Sybil said, "I have an important meeting."

"One more thing," Maizy said. "We're trying to find Dusty Rose."

Sybil ignored her. "I'm expecting the funeral director."

I stared at her. "You haven't buried Oxnard yet?" Was she shopping for a bargain or something?

"Of course I buried him," she snapped. "Now I need to pay the man for giving Oxie a proper send-off. I went with a white theme. White hearse, white flowers, white casket. I never understood black at funerals. It's so bleak."

"Do you know where Dusty Rose lives?" Maizy asked.

Sybil wasn't done. "I even got a discount on a white suit, since I only needed the front half of it. Oxie didn't even wear pants; I kept the bottom half of the casket closed. He would have loved it."

She had just inherited millions thanks to incontinent adults everywhere, and she'd buried her husband in a napkin?

On second thought, he probably *would* have loved it.

"Maybe you should have considered cremation," I suggested.

"Oxie was afraid of fire," she said. "Of course, he was afraid of being buried alive, too. And boxer shorts."

Ewww.

She shook her head. "Maybe I should have filed him in one of those mausoleums. Or do you think that's a little too public housing?"

"Why didn't you go green?" Maizy said. "You could've put him through the wood chipper, and used him to mulch the garden."

Sybil didn't even flinch. "The HOA would never have gone for it. But I could still move him to the penthouse drawer. You can't leave flowers, but let's be honest, how many times am I going to visit him anyway?"

"You must have really loved him," I said.

"I married him, didn't I?" she asked.

I'd seen a warmer union between hamsters.

"What can you tell us about Dusty Rose?" Maizy asked. "We'd like to talk to her."

"I can't tell you anything about her," Sybil said. "Oxie found her and hired her."

"And diddled her?" Maizy asked.

Sybil stared at her. "I think it's time for you to leave." She yanked the door open.

Outside, a gleaming black Lincoln was pulling into the driveway. The funeral home director. And behind the Lincoln, a Mercedes sedan with Herman Kantz behind the wheel. A ginormous arrangement of red roses rode shotgun.

I turned to Sybil. "Nice of Herman Kantz to pay his respects personally."

"He was Oxie's financial adviser," Sybil said, as if that explained everything. "Thank you for stopping by."

"We'll come back later," Maizy whispered to me.

"Don't even think about coming back later," Sybil told us. "The neighbors keep a close eye on the place."

"I'm not worried about a bunch of blue-hairs," Maizy whispered.

"And then there's the security patrol," Sybil said. "They have guns. But don't worry, they won't shoot you."

"I'm not worried about some rent-a-cops," Maizy whispered.

"They'd rather sic the dogs on intruders," Sybil said. "Less paperwork."

"Our business here is done," Maizy said.

CHAPTER TWENTY-SEVEN

———

"That woman is a goober," Maizy said when we were back in the Bentley. This time she was driving. I was okay with it if Honest Aaron was. Even if Maizy had a tendency to consider red lights on a case-by-case basis.

"I was thinking of another word," I said. "But we can go with goober. Question is, did the goober commit murder."

Maizy whipped out her cell phone and snapped a couple photos of David as we drove past him. From the good side. "She's obfuscating."

I nodded gravely, like I knew what that meant. And wondering if I should have taken some pictures, too, since that might be my last visit to Oxnard's house. Then I remembered the Rod Rockstone photo in my bag. Close enough.

"I mean," Maizy said, "who doesn't know if their partner can swim? I know my parents can swim. I know Uncle Curt can swim. I know you can swim."

I grimaced. "I'm not swimming until it's socially acceptable to do it in full sweats." *SI*'s swimsuit edition wouldn't be calling me anytime soon.

"That's just your negative self-image," Maizy said. "I keep meaning to talk to you about that."

We sailed past the gatehouse and through the open gate.

"There's no hope for me," I said. "Save yourself."

"Don't you worry," Maizy said cheerfully. "I'm just fine. My point is, family knows things like that, don't they? Maybe she knew Oxnard couldn't, so she shoved him in the pool and went to collect his money."

"But," I said, "the will hasn't been officially redrafted yet, as far as I know."

"But does Sybil know that?" Maizy asked.

I couldn't see how she would. Not like she'd had to sign it. She may have assumed it, and that would be just as dangerous for Oxnard.

I suddenly remembered something. "The contracts!"

Maizy glanced over at me. "Huh?"

"Remember the contracts I saw in Oxnard's office? I was hoping to take another look at them."

"What's the problem? You read them, right?"

Depended how you defined *read*. I'd seen some names and dollar figures. Beyond that, it had been a lot of boring legalese. Kind of like a day at the office.

"Of course I read them," I said. "I'm a highly trained legal professional."

"Okay," Maizy said. "So what were they about?"

"Not a clue," I said.

"I know what your problem is," she said. "You need to improve your brain's plasticity. I hear that gingko biloba is good for memory loss."

"It's not memory loss," I snapped. "I saw it one time, and I didn't think it was important enough to memorize."

"Everything's important enough to memorize," she said. "Maybe you should start taking pictures when we're investigating. You know, so you don't keep forgetting things."

"You're just showing off because you have an eidetic memory," I said. "And were those pictures you just took back there part of the investigation?"

She shrugged. "That was scouting. Herbie Hairston is looking for some statuary."

The juvenile delinquent in Maizy's class and frequent supplier of questionable goods. Herbie was the reason I'd wound up with zip ties, a shovel, and a bag of lime in the trunk of my car. If they'd all come used, I wasn't going to be the one to rat him out.

"Herbie Hairston lives with his parents," I snapped. At least until he moved into the county jail.

"That's the point," Maizy said. "Their anniversary is coming up. He wants to get them something nice. I think it's sweet."

"They live in an apartment!" I said.

"Don't judge," Maizy told me.

I sighed. If Herbie Hairston wanted to steal Incontinent David, that was his business. Maybe he could steal a wet vac while he was at it.

Maizy coasted through a stop sign and around a corner. "Maybe we should hypnotize you," she said. "People remember all kinds of things under hypnosis. It's not even that hard. I Googled it."

"I don't think so," I said. "You might make me do something stupid every time I hear a bell ring or something. Besides, I don't think you can learn how to hypnotize someone from the internet."

"Are you kidding?" she said. "You can learn *anything* on the internet. But if you want to do everything the hard way, we'll just sneak back in when Sybil's out having her teeth sharpened and—"

"Let's give it a shot," I said.

* * *

"Dude, you need to relax," Maizy said.

"I *am* relaxed," I told her, surprised that my pants didn't spontaneously burst into flames. Of *course* I wasn't relaxed. Even though we were at my apartment, the lights were low, and the nubs of my emergency candles were flickering, throwing off the delectable scent of vanilla, my nerves buzzed as if I'd mainlined a gallon of caffeine. The ambiance had, however, put Ashley to sleep immediately. She was curled up in the recliner on top of Maizy's hoodie, snoring gently. To be fair, Ashley slept about twenty-two hours a day, so it might have been less ambiance and more narcolepsy.

"Breathe," Maizy told me. She sat in front of me cross-legged, gazing earnestly into my eyes. "This won't work if you don't breathe."

"I told you," I said, "I can't be hypnotized. I don't believe in it."

"Yeah, I heard you," Maizy said. "But you'll change your mind once you get on the hypnotic staircase."

"Hypnotic staircase," I repeated. "That sounds made up."

Ashley cracked open one eye and gave me a *Will you be quiet? You're disturbing my nap* glare. Ashley was a very advanced cat.

Maizy rolled her eyes. "Who's the expert here?"

"Beats me," I said.

"Look," she said. "You want to remember the names on the contracts, but because you're old, you can't. It's like my grampy when he has to pee in the middle of the night. So we can either sneak back into Oxnard's house, or you can start concentrating on this." And she held up the Rod Rockstone trading card.

My mouth fell open. "Where'd that come from?"

"I think we both know the answer to that," Maizy said.

It was the first time Rod had seen the light of day since I'd pilfered him from Oxnard's office. Well, except for that time I'd sneaked a peek in my car at the red light on the way home. And in the conference room, a couple or dozen times when I'd been having especially rough days at work.

Okay, so Rod had been hanging out more than tweens at a Taylor Swift concert.

"Now just let your eyes follow the bouncing stud." She started tipping the card back and forth, very slowly, as if it was the swinging pendulum from every clichéd hypnosis scene ever created. Only this was better, because Rod's pendulum was more fun to focus on.

"This is completely inappropriate," I told her.

Maizy kept tilting the card right, then left, right, then left. "Why?"

"Because you're using up my emergency candles," I said. "Why do you think?"

"You don't need them," Maizy said. "You have Uncle Curt. He's got flashlights. Anyway, don't be such a prude. It's not like the dude's totally naked." She glanced at the card. Rod was barely wearing a tan line. Just the Speedo that wasn't up to the job. "Can I borrow this?" she asked.

"No, you can't borrow it," I snapped.

"Whatever," she said. "*God.* Come on, take some deep breaths in through your mouth and out through your nose, real slow. Four counts in, eight counts out. Focus on relaxing your muscles one at a time. Start with your toes."

I rolled my eyes. "How am I supposed to relax my toes?"

"Stop clenching," Maizy said. "I can tell you're clenching. Straighten them out. Now your ankles."

"I have very tense ankles," I told her.

She ignored me. "And your calves."

"My calves have been under a lot of stress lately," I said.

"Forget the muscles," she said. "Imagine you're on the top step of a staircase, about to take a step down. Every step down will make you more relaxed."

"What's at the bottom?" I asked. "Are there spiders?"

"No spiders," she said. "Just mellowness. Take another step down now. And another. All the stress stays behind you while you go farther into relaxation. Down one more step."

"Is this the hyp..." I started to say, but then the words kind of drifted away from me and I felt a weird sort of calm overtake me. I settled into it. My shoulders felt loose. My body felt light. I think my toes even relaxed. If I'd believed in hypnosis, this is what I'd imagined it to be.

"Think about Oxnard's office," Maizy said. "You went through his papers. You found contracts."

I nodded. "No Flows, Incorporated."

"What were the names on the contracts?"

"No Flows, Incorporated," I said.

"The other names," she said.

"There weren't any," I said. "They weren't signed."

"Who was supposed to sign them?" she said. "*God*," she muttered under her breath.

I stared into middle space, picturing the office, the ginormous desk, the contracts, the pages of tiny print ending in signature lines. I could picture it as easily and vividly as if I held it in my hands. "Jalen Jefferson. Allison Madeline Cartwright. Caroline Kirby."

"Do those names mean anything to you?"

"Not a thing."

"Me, neither," she said. "Did you see anything else?"

I thought about it. "Yes. A scary picture of Abigail and Alston. His eyes follow you when you move, like that picture at the Haunted Mansion at Disney." I didn't want to think about Alston's eyes following me. It creeped me out a little. If he was forty years younger, it would creep me out a lot. He had those kind of eyes. Vulture eyes. Oxnard's eyes.

Maizy was frowning at me. "Anything else?"

I dragged my focus back to Oxnard's office. "An invoice from Lizette Larue for the wedding."

"Okay," she said. "How much was it for?"

"Forty thousand dollars," I said. "And eighty-two cents." She blinked. "Seriously?"

"I know, right?" I said. "For a sappy CD and some folding chairs."

"What a waste," Maizy said.

I nodded my agreement. "All that filet mignon."

"I meant the money," Maizy said. "What a waste of money."

Oh.

"Yeah," I said. "I meant that, too."

"Do you remember anything else?" she asked.

I shook my head. "Yes," I said suddenly. "The pictures."

"What pictures? Who's in the pictures?"

I could feel a goofy smile stretch my lips. "*He* is. There were others, but he was the best."

Maizy stared at me. "We're still talking about Oxnard's office, right?"

"He's very flexible," I added. "Just look at him."

"Sure he is," Maizy said. "I see him right over there in the corner. Can you remember anything else besides your imaginary friend?"

"He had a big desk," I said. "That's all."

"Yeah," Maizy said. "All guys say that."

I stewed in my mellowness for a minute or two. Then my thoughts drifted over to Curt, and my grin got bigger because Curt was *real*. And that got me wondering what he was doing, and whether or not he was flexible. All signs pointed to yes.

"Whatever you're doing right now," Maizy said, "stop it. We're not done here. Concentrate."

We went back and forth for awhile, Maizy trying to extract a little more information from me, and me coming up empty. I just hadn't seen anything to remember beyond the names, and the names meant nothing to either one of us. Thing is, I didn't seem to care. I just wanted to float along in that mellow space for as long as I could. This was the meditative state that yoga kept promising me I would attain but never had.

"I think we're done here," Maizy said finally. "Come on back up the stairs, slowly. With each step you'll—"

"But I don't want to come back," I said.

"You have to," she said. "We have work to do. Walk up another step."

"I think Rod's gone," I said.

"Whatever," Maizy said. "*Get up the steps!*"

I snapped out of my mellowness instantly, blinked a couple of times, and said, "Where'd Rod go?"

"I must've skipped something," Maizy muttered.

I narrowed my eyes at her. "He's in your pocket, isn't he?"

Maizy shoved a handful of blue hair out of her eyes. "Forget about Rod. We have work to do. Do you feel alright?"

Someone knocked on my door.

"Bok bok," I said.

"Uh-oh," Maizy said.

My eyes got wide. "What was that?"

"Nothing," she said. "Someone's at the door. I'll go see who it is." She hurried away and came back a few seconds later with Lizette Larue. Lizette was wearing a perfectly tailored red pantsuit with sky-high heels that gave her four more inches of height. She'd lost the pink laptop but gained a carryon-sized leather handbag looped over her left forearm.

"I'm looking for Sybil Thorpe," she said. "I thought you might know where she is, since you were her maid of honor."

I ignored her.

"What did you do to me?" I asked Maizy.

"Little experiment," she said. "Guess I don't know my own strength."

"Want to find out mine?" I asked. "You've got to do something!"

"You just need a little tweak," she said. "No big deal."

"Hello?" Lizette stomped her little foot a few times to get my attention. "Did you hear me?"

"Bok bok," I said, and rolled my eyes.

Lizette stared at me.

"Okay," she said, "I get it. I was a witch. I treated you badly. But that woman made me want to kill someone."

Interesting choice of words.

"Did you?" Maizy cut in. "Kill someone, I mean?"

Lizette's eyes got big with indignation. "Of course not. I can't believe you would ask me that. Who are you, anyway?"

"Not important," Maizy said. "Just wanted to put it out there. Come in, sit down. Let me take your suitcase." She unhitched the bag from Lizette's arm and dropped it on the floor with a thud.

"Bok bok," I said.

"Why does she keep doing that?" Lizette asked Maizy.

"It's just a thing," Maizy said with a shrug.

"A *big* thing," I added with a touch of hostility, because I'd just *known* something like this was going to happen. And I had only myself to blame.

"So where'd you go after the wedding?" Maizy asked her.

Lizette grimaced. "I went to the closest bar and had a few drinks. I wanted to forget the whole affair."

"Me, too," Maizy said. "Especially the part where the groom died."

"That was awful," Lizette agreed. "I wouldn't be surprised if that model did it. She was really mad at Mr. Thorpe."

I remembered that. "Do you know why?"

"Some business deal or other, I think," she said. "It sounded like Mr. Thorpe had deceived her in some way. Of course, I didn't hear the whole conversation. I was busy working for free."

Lizette glanced at the recliner where Ashley had rousted herself into a sitting position and was watching us with unblinking eyes. "Look, I don't know what I can say besides I'm sorry," she told us. "But I'd reached my limit after dealing with Sybil. I shouldn't have even taken the job. I should have listened to my instincts when I heard her making plans for when the old goat was gone. That's what she called him."

Lizette seemed to eavesdrop more than a wiretap.

"Plans?" Maizy repeated. "What do you mean? Who was she talking to?"

"I don't know," she said. "She was on the phone. I just heard bits and pieces before she realized I was there and hung up."

"What pieces did you hear?" Maizy asked.

Lizette thought for a second. "I'm sorry, I don't remember."

"I can help you with that," Maizy said.

I flung myself off the couch. "No!"

They both looked at me.

"What I mean," I said, "is did she mention anything about killing her husband?"

"Maybe." Lizette did a little headshake. "I don't want to say, really. I don't know. I don't even remember much of it, to be honest with you. She started screaming at me and it made me so anxious, I just wanted to leave. Anyway." She reached into her bag for a cream-colored envelope with pretty cursive writing on its face. "I really just stopped by to see if you could get this in front of her. I did every little silly thing she asked, and now she doesn't want to pay me."

I was starting to think the wrong Thorpe had been killed. Sybil seemed to have ticked off even more people than Oxnard.

"Did you leave bills here before?" I asked her.

Lizette nodded. "You threw them out, right? I don't blame you. Why would you want to help me get paid?"

I wanted everyone to get paid, starting with me. Unfortunately for Lizette, Sybil hadn't seen it the same way.

"I went to her house," Lizette was saying. "And Pandora told me she wasn't there. I think she's hiding from me." She laid the envelope on my coffee table. "Tell her she has ten days to pay it before I get my lawyer involved."

Maizy scooped up the envelope. "I'll take care of this. Do you have a card?"

Lizette shook her head. "I'm sorry. I don't have one on me. Are you planning a wedding?"

"God, no," Maizy said. "I'm never getting married. I meant for your lawyer."

Lizette seemed vaguely confused. "Why do you need that?"

Maizy shrugged. "You never know what may happen. It's good to have a lawyer on speed dial. It's a real time saver."

Lizette glanced at me. "Is she serious?"

"She likes to plan ahead," I said.

"Well." She glanced at both of us. "I'd appreciate anything you can do. And again, for what it's worth, I'm sorry for the way I treated you."

"I appreciate that," I said.

"I'll show you the door," Maizy told her. She took a step to the left and pointed. "There it is."

Lizette's eyebrows puckered for a second before she picked up her bag and let herself out, letting the door bang shut behind her.

"What'd you think of *that*?" Maizy asked.

"Bok bok," I said.

CHAPTER TWENTY-EIGHT

———

Curt showed up a half hour later, after Maizy had tweaked my inner chickcn. He was carrying a carpet sample which he tossed on the coffee table. "Cam wants this one. What do you think?"

"You should've been here sooner," Maizy told him. "You missed the wedding planner."

"Seen it," Curt said. "Not a fan."

I picked up the sample. "She means Lizette Larue," I said. "Sybil's wedding planner. She stopped by to apologize and drop off her bill." I hesitated. "Mostly to drop off her bill. She wants me to convince Sybil to pay it."

He scooped Ashley up with one hand and sat in the recliner, kicked the footrest up, and deposited her in his lap. She kneaded his thigh for thirty seconds and settled in, purring violently. "And you're supposed to do this how?" he asked.

"Maybe convince isn't the right word," I said. "Maybe suggest is a better one."

"I say you mail it to her," Curt said. "Anonymously. It's not your problem."

"We should probably take it over there," Maizy said. "Seeing as how Lizette heard Sybil on the phone making plans for life after Oxnard."

"The guy was almost a hundred," Curt said. "Not exactly a stretch that there'd be life after Oxnard."

Maizy's cell phone buzzed with an incoming text. She whipped it out of the pocket of her hoodie and checked the screen. "Little complication. Remember Antoine said Herman wasn't at the country club on the sixteenth?"

I nodded.

"Who's Antoine?" Curt asked.

"Turns out Antoine wasn't working on the night of the sixteenth," Maizy said. "He swapped nights so another chef, Giorgio, could go to his sister's wedding."

"So we still don't know if Herman was there on the night of the murder," I said. "He might have been. Do you know Giorgio?"

Maizy shook her head. "I don't know Gil, either. But we probably shouldn't show up in the kitchen there anymore. Someone complained to the Board of Health. They found a hair in their vichyssoise."

"Let me guess," Curt said. "It was blue."

"I don't see the problem," Maizy said. "Vichyssoise could use a little color."

I rolled my eyes.

"So let me see if I get this," he said. "Three guys named Antoine, Giorgio, and Gil work at the country club and none of them know if Herman Kantz showed up there on the night Oxnard was killed, and you guys didn't bother to cover your hair when you trampled through their kitchen."

"That's pretty much it," I told him. "Except Giorgio and Gil might know. We didn't talk to them."

Maizy glanced up from her cell phone. "And we won't be, either. I'm not putting a stupid shower cap on for anyone. It takes a lot of work to look like me."

I'd heard that before, and I'd seen how much work it had taken. I'd spent more time blinking. I held up the carpet sample. "This is nice."

"You think?" He studied it. "It won't match the walls."

"The walls need painting," I told him. In truth, he'd given me the green light when I'd moved in to redecorate. I'd just never gotten around to it. I'd never found the time with my high-powered job and my demanding sleep schedule. "And then the drapes probably won't match," I added. "Not that that's your responsibility. Except I might need new hardware, and you'd have to install that." Preferably shirtless.

Curt shook his head. "It's like I'm married."

"I hate to interrupt this boring conversation," Maizy cut in. "But I need to get to the nearest pharmacy before they close."

She did a sidelong glance in Curt's direction. "And I can't drive myself, since I only have my permit."

That, and the phony driver's license tucked in her backpack.

"Please tell me you're not buying a home pregnancy test," Curt said.

"Something much more important," Maizy said.

"Penicillin?" he asked.

"Sometimes I don't think you get me," Maizy told him.

"Pretty sure I never will," he said.

* * *

Twenty minutes later I followed Maizy into the pharmacy and thankfully, into the cosmetics aisle, where I people-watched while she compared black eyeliners. To be honest, I tried to stay out of cosmetics departments. I had enough self-confidence issues without bright lights and magnifying mirrors.

It didn't take long for me to notice Dusty Rose farther down the aisle, fabulous in an electric blue dress and hair that shone like glass.

I tapped Maizy on the shoulder. "Maize, look."

Maizy looked. "Isn't that Bridesmaid Number Two?"

"Otherwise known as Dusty Rose," I said. "The one deceived by Oxnard. I'm going to go talk to her."

"I'll be right there," she said. "As soon as I find an eyeliner that doesn't have petroleum in it."

"Good luck with that," I told her.

Up close, Dusty wasn't so fabulous. In fact, she was downright imperfect. Her arms and legs and chest were splotchy with a bright pink rash, and I noticed she was clutching a tube of concealer. One wasn't going to be enough.

She noticed that I noticed. "I'm sort of having a little issue." She tugged at the hem of her dress to pull it down over her thighs but that was like trying to cover a Ferrari with a handkerchief.

I tried not to stare. "Have you seen a doctor?"

She nodded. "He says it's stress related. I'm having some money problems right now."

"I'm sorry to hear it," I said. "Didn't you say you had landed a job?"

A middle-aged woman with wiry graying hair and mom jeans charged up the aisle. She hesitated when she saw Dusty, and I could practically see the *Why bother* thought bubble hovering over her head.

Dusty didn't notice. "I lost it."

Hm. "What happened?" I asked.

A shadow darkened her face. "You want to know what happened? Oxnard Thorpe was a pervert!"

Tell me something I didn't know.

"Can you be more specific?" I asked.

"He promised me the spokesmodel position at No Flows if…" She hesitated, blushing.

"I think I get it," I said. Clearly Oxnard's libido had been half his age.

"It's hard out there," Dusty said. "There's a lot of beautiful girls. So I did. Once." She shuddered.

"He didn't tell you he'd sold the company," I guessed.

"Worse than that," she said. "He filmed us. And he was trying to *sell* the video!"

"Who'd want to see that?" Too late, I realized I'd been thinking aloud. "Sorry. I didn't mean—"

"You're right," Dusty said. "He was a disgusting man."

"Excuse me." The woman approached us clutching two lipsticks. "Which color do you think is best for me?"

"You don't want either one," Dusty told her. "These will dry out your lips. Go with the hydrating lipstick." She tilted her head, assessing the woman's face. "In a nice rosy shade. It'll complement your hair color."

I agreed. Pink did go well with gray. When I had Dusty's attention again, I asked, "When did Oxnard tell you this?"

"After the wedding." Her voice was flat. "When I was helping him pick breadstick crumbs out of his tuxedo."

Yuck.

"That must have been a surprise," I said.

"A surprise?" She snorted. "You could say that. It's also a surprise that my furniture doesn't fit underneath the overpass where I'll be living soon."

Oh, boy. Was that motive I heard?

"Are things that bad?" I asked.

"Not if I want a job as a cashier. Maybe I can live in Oxnard's office. That'd be ironic, wouldn't it?"

I blinked. "What office?"

"He kept a place in Maple Grove," she said. "I don't think he ever told his wife."

Which probably meant he kept things there that he wanted to remain hidden. Which seemed like pretty much everything except his winkie.

She shook her head. "I'm sorry, I shouldn't have said anything. Everyone's got problems, right?"

Sure. But not everyone solved them with murder.

Her nose wrinkled. "Here," she said to the woman, "let me help you." She pointed. "Try this one." She pointed again. "And this one."

"You and Oxnard seemed to get along so well," I said, thinking aloud.

"Thanks to acting lessons," she said.

Given what she'd told me, she'd have to be Meryl Streep.

Was she a good enough actress to lure Oxnard to the pool for a grand seduction so she could shove him off the edge to his death? I had two thoughts about that. One was that it wouldn't take much to lure Oxnard anywhere, and another was *Eww*. Nobody could be *that* good an actress. Of course, homelessness may have made her desperate, and being exploited could have made her vengeful.

Maizy stomped down the aisle in her Doc Martens, clearly aggravated. "Looks like if I don't want to buy poison makeup, I have to go to the health food store."

The middle-aged woman glanced over with alarm.

"That'll teach me to think positive," Maizy grumbled. She stuck her hands on her hips. "So what are you guys talking about?"

No point in embarrassing Dusty with the video.

"Dusty lost a spokesmodel job," I said. "For No Flows."

"Maybe it's that rash," Maizy said.

Dusty's cheeks pinkened. "It's from stress."

"You need to eliminate stress," Maizy told her. "And wear pants."

"I'm working on it," Dusty told her. "I thought I had everything under control and it kind of blew up on me."

"That'll happen," Maizy said. "You know, I hear killing people can be stressful."

I shot her a warning look. "So where'd you go after the wedding, anyway?" I asked Dusty. "Everyone cleared out so fast, I didn't even get a chance to say goodbye."

She shrugged. "I went home to bed. While I still have a home and a bed. I should've kept my date. He was going to fly me to his place in Kennebunkport for the weekend. Last time he had lobsters and champagne waiting." She smiled a little, reminiscing.

Same old Saturday night to me.

"What's she mean?" Maizy asked me. She turned to Dusty. "You mean you weren't doing nicky-nack with the geezer?"

"Hey, I only did that once," Dusty said.

"She's an actress, too," I told Maizy.

"Aren't we all?" Maizy said.

I felt my teeth grind. "I mean she's taking acting lessons."

"She needs lessons to fool a guy?" Maizy asked. "It's the easiest thing in the world. They *want* to be fooled. They practically *ask* for it."

"I don't want to fool Raul," Dusty said.

"You say that now," Maizy told her. "Wait till Raul eats a few more lobsters and puts on thirty pounds and clogs a couple arteries."

Dusty looked at me. "I don't understand her."

"No one does," I said. "So listen, I'm sure you heard that Oxnard is dead."

A trace of a smile dusted her lips and was gone. "I'm not surprised someone killed him."

Maizy and I traded glances.

"Who said someone killed him?" I asked.

"That's what I was told," she said.

Well, that couldn't be more vague.

"Any idea who might have wanted him dead?" I asked. *Besides you?*

Dusty shrugged. "Pick a card. That man had more shady deals going than you can imagine. I mean, take Triple D Supply. His adviser told him he was diversifying into another multimillion-dollar industry. But those books weren't just cooked, they were burnt."

"Herman Kantz?" I asked.

Dusty shrugged. "I guess so. Oxnard trusted that guy because *she* recommended him."

Something prickled up my spine. "She who?"

"Sybil, of course."

"What's Triple D Supply?" Maizy asked. I could practically see thought bubbles forming over her head.

Dusty smirked. "It's a joke. Funny, right?"

"I've got to go call someone," Maizy told me. "Meet you at the car."

I suddenly remembered the paperwork I'd seen on Oxnard's desk. "Wait a minute," I said. "Are you sure you'd gotten that job in the first place? I saw some contracts with the names Allison Cartwright and Caroline Kirby on them."

Dusty smiled. "You didn't think anyone was actually named Dusty Rose, did you?"

Only if she was lucky.

"I'm Caroline Kirby," she said. "And yes, Oxnard told me I had a job on a two-year contract, for six figures. And now I can sell lipstick."

I didn't know what to say. Dusty's anger practically radiated off her. "Are you saying he drew up phony contracts?" I asked.

"Is that so hard to believe?" Dusty asked. "Did you notice he never signed them?"

As a matter of fact, I had.

"It was all a game to him." Bitterness soured her voice. "My life was just a game to him."

The middle-aged woman stepped into the silence to ask, "Is this better?" She puckered her lips at Dusty.

"What?" Dusty gave a start. "I—no. No. Let me help you." With the efficiency of a surgeon, she painted a set of curvaceous lips on the woman. "There. Better."

The woman beamed at herself in the mirror. Then she beamed at Dusty. Which led me to an epiphany.

"You should be working as a makeup artist," I told her. "You know, as soon as your problem clears up. I bet you could build a client base in no time."

"You think?" I could tell she was intrigued by the idea. That homicidal glint in her eyes had all but disappeared.

"I really do," I said. As long as she wasn't thrown in jail for killing Oxnard.

"Yeah." I could practically see the gears chugging away while she thought about it. "Yeah," she said again. "I think I'll look into that. Tell you what, you can be my first client. You could use a head-to-toe makeover."

Me and my big mouth.

CHAPTER TWENTY-NINE

———

"Well, this isn't going to get us anywhere," I said two nights later when we rolled to a stop in what used to be the parking lot of Triple D Supply in Elmer Landing, a tiny industrial town on the banks of the Delaware River. The lot was strewn with litter and broken glass, choked with weeds, and it was still in better shape than the warehouse, which had been gutted by fire. Most of the windows and a large part of the roof were gone.

"Herman Kantz strikes again," Maizy muttered. Her backpack was open on the floor at her feet. Her tablet was in her lap.

A tugboat inched its way up the river toward the old Philadelphia Navy Yard. "What does that mean?"

She pointed to the screen. "He used to be majority owner of this dump. Triple D filed for bankruptcy in 2015."

Yet he'd recommended it to Oxnard as an investment? Another black mark on Herman's résumé. And Oxnard had taken the bait. Herman Kantz didn't strike me as that persuasive, unless Sybil had gotten involved.

Which brought me back to Sybil's relationship with Herman Kantz. Whatever it might be, it was strong enough to warrant red roses and private visits.

I restarted the car, and we drove out of the lot toward home.

"I'm not sure where to go with this," I said.

"I've got more bad news," Maizy said. "Bitsy Dolman hasn't paid her electric bill in four months." She grinned. "Told you."

"Okay," I said. "So she's having a hard time right now."

"*Hard time* is not having money for Starbucks," Maizy said. "What she's having is Chapter 13. I feel kind of bad for her."

"She still might have killed Oxnard," I reminded her. "And she did lie about attending that Fire and Ice fashion show on the night of the wedding."

"What was she gonna do?" Maizy asked. "Admit that she ran home alone to her rat hole in Loserville?"

"That's kind of harsh," I said. "You don't know that she was alone."

"Maybe we should send her a flashlight," Maizy said. "A small one, so she wouldn't have to see very much. Besides, how do we know that she lied?"

"You saw her house, right?" I said.

"Sloppy houses don't necessarily imply poverty," Maizy said.

In my case, it came uncomfortably close.

"I think it's worth a phone call," she said.

"I checked the flight schedules," I said. "There weren't any planes leaving Philly for Chicago at that time of night."

"So maybe she used a private jet."

"Oh, sure," I said. "I don't know how I missed it. She must have had it parked out back next to limousine and the yacht."

"You're judging again," Maizy said. "Keep an open mind. How many old women have died with a million dollars in a jelly jar in the fridge behind the Lactaid and gross white bread?"

I gave her a look. "I told you, I don't like whole grains."

"I didn't mean that personally," she said. "But it's interesting that you went there."

"Wait a minute," I said. "The wedding was over by 9:30. She disappeared after the food fight right afterwards. The airport is a twenty-minute drive. And Chicago is less than a two-hour flight. Which would have put her there at midnight, no matter if she flew commercial or sprouted wings."

"True," Maizy said. "Except what if the fashion show wasn't on Saturday, but on Sunday, and she flew out Saturday night? Did she actually say it was held on Saturday night? Because that would be a big fat lie."

I couldn't remember. And I wasn't risking hypnosis again. "Better make the call," I told her.

Maizy did an internet search, whipped out another cell phone from her hoodie, and punched in the number. "I just bought more minutes," she told me. Like I wasn't used to Maizy owning more cell phones than AT&T. A second later, she said, "I'd like to speak to whoever handles orders from the Fire and Ice show." Pause. "Yes, I know it's over." Pause. "Not interested." Pause. "Seriously, not interested." Pause. "Will you get off it? *God.*"

I nudged her. "Take it easy."

She covered the phone. "Like I'd buy an $8,000 bra and panty set."

I nodded my agreement. No way I'd do that, either. Unless the panties were made of cashmere and the bra came with preinstalled cleavage. Hm.

"Any wiggle room on that price?" I whispered.

Maizy didn't hear me. She was back on the phone. "This is Angelica from Dolman Personal Shopping," she said. "Bitsy Dolman hasn't received her order from this year's show, and she has a client waiting for it." Another pause. "Don't ask me. I don't know what she ordered. I'm just supposed to find out what happened to the shipment. I'll hold, but only if you don't assault me with Muzak."

I poked her in the ribs. "Don't be rude."

"I think I'm being incredibly tolerant under the circumstances," she said. "Have you ever heard Muzak?"

Yeah, alright, she had a point.

About thirty seconds later, she sat up straighter. "What do you mean, she wasn't there this year? She's been going for fifteen years." She listened for a few seconds. "Yes, I know the show's only been held for nine. That's my point. Bitsy's ahead of the curve." She listened for a few more seconds and hung up. "She didn't go."

Big surprise. "What'd they say?" I asked. "Why not?"

"They don't know," Maizy said. "She just dropped out of sight about six months ago."

"Maybe we ought to revisit Bitsy," I said.

"While we're at it," Maizy said, "we ought to find out more about Dusty. I might like her, but I didn't hear any alibi back there. Just a lot of 'should've kept that date with Mortimer Moneybags and his magic Cessna'."

"Agreed," I said. "But wouldn't the killer had to have known about the hidden hallway to stay out of sight till everyone left?"

Maizy rolled her eyes. "Let me ask you something. Did you know where in the house I was while you were snarfing dinner?"

"No," I said. "And I've been meaning to talk to you about that."

"My point," Maizy said, ignoring me, "is it's a big house. Lots of hidey-holes." She pushed hair out of her eyes. "It was a good thought, though. You're getting better at this."

"It sure doesn't feel that way," I said.

CHAPTER THIRTY

––––––

Friday night, I came awake with a start and realized the phone was ringing. I grabbed it before it disturbed Ashley, who was snoozing comfortably on top of my head. "What?"

"So there I was tonight," Sybil said, as if we'd been chatting away for hours, "a grieving widow in the house that was rightfully mine, and what do you suppose happened?"

"Can't this wait till morning?" I asked, yawning. Outside, a light rain was falling. It was 2:15 a.m. "How did you get my number?"

"Abigail and Alston happened," she went on, ignoring me. "They seem to think the house is theirs now."

"Yeah," I said. "I noticed that."

There was a beat of silence. "You talked to them?"

"Of course," I said. "I'm a detective." Why did it sound better when Maizy said it? "Abigail seems pretty anxious to have the will probated. Does she know something you don't?"

"I didn't marry him for his money," Sybil said. "If that's what you're asking."

I'm sure it hadn't soured the deal.

"Am I right in thinking Abigail controls the household?" I asked.

Sybil snorted. "Don't most women?"

I wouldn't know about that. But I was pleased to learn that my instincts were dead on. Now the question was what to do about them. I couldn't forget Abigail's hostility, or their little drama at the pharmacy. And they might have had a rich brother, but it didn't seem that Oxnard had shared the wealth. Instead, he'd put them even farther from the easy life by marrying Sybil. I wondered if he'd cut them off entirely, and if he had, had Sybil put him up to it?

"Abby talked to the police," she was saying.

I sat up against the pillows, causing Ashley to wake up and jump off the bed with a little *Mrrreww* of protest. "What?"

"She's trying to convince them I killed Oxie. Nothing would make her happier than to see me in jail."

"Why would she do that?"

Her tone was withering. "People get railroaded all the time. It's not that hard to do when you have money behind your name."

I didn't think Abigail Thorpe had much of anything behind her name, but maybe the name was enough. And the desire for revenge.

But Abigail Thorpe wasn't the only suspect. Just the oldest one.

"Speaking of money," I said, "what can you tell me about Bitsy Dolman?"

Sybil snorted. "Those two things don't belong in the same sentence."

Yeah, I'd figured out that much.

"Bitsy's best years were about two decades ago," Sybil said. "She ran through her money and lost her looks. If Oxie hadn't insisted, that woman wouldn't have been within a mile of my wedding."

"But why did Oxie insist?" I asked. "She seemed so different from the other guests."

"My husband had a very warm heart," she said. "He said they were childhood friends or some such nonsense."

Her sentimentality was staggering.

"Bitsy Dolman isn't important," Sybil said. "You need to do something about Abigail Thorpe. Can't you threaten her with a slander suit or something?"

"Do you really want to sue your sister-in-law?" I asked. "When she just lost her brother?"

"I just lost my husband," she snapped. "Does she care about my feelings?"

I sighed. "I'll talk to Howard about it. Where can I get ahold of you?"

"I'll find you," she said, and hung up.

Now why did that sound like a threat?

CHAPTER THIRTY-ONE

———

Maizy showed up at 4:45 on Monday, just as a deposition was breaking up in the conference room, and slouched into the chair behind the empty desk to wait for five.

"How was school?" I asked her.

She shrugged. "Same old. I'm just putting in my time to satisfy the man."

"Who's the man?" Missy asked.

"Her father," I said.

A minute later, Eunice staggered into the room with pale cheeks and glazed eyes. I hadn't seen her all day, and I hadn't missed much. Brown and beige, air of quiet desperation. Pretty standard for Eunice.

"Is that what it's like?" She fanned herself with her legal pad. The page was full of doodles "That was pure hell. All that bickering and outright lying. And *that* was only the lawyers." She shuddered.

"Welcome to the wonderful world of the law," I told her. "I can't imagine why you wanted to be part of it."

"But since you did," Missy said, "might as well enjoy the benefits."

"Are there any?" Eunice asked.

Missy nodded. "Bakery goods. Have a leftover doughnut."

"I knew I wouldn't be any good at this," Eunice moaned. "I can't even keep my office right. Howard told me I had to get it in order by the end of the week." She glanced around for a place to sit, and saw Maizy. "Hey," she said.

"Hey," Maizy said cheerfully. "How goes the ambulance chasing?"

Eunice let out a tortured sigh. "Not so good. Everyone's been obeying stop signs and yellow lights lately."

"Bummer," Maizy said. "Don't worry, sooner or later there'll be a cleanup in aisle five and someone will slip and fall in it."

Eunice considered it. "That's a good point. Thanks."

"No thanks necessary," Maizy said. "It's what I do."

"Last call for doughnuts." Missy waved the plate around. "Guaranteed to ease your suffering."

Eunice snatched two of them.

"Want to do a mock summation?" I asked her. "Might help you de-stress."

"Are you kidding? If I hear any more legalese today, my head may explode." She ate a chocolate frosted in three bites. "It sure isn't like *Boston Legal* around here," she said.

"Nothing's ever what it seems to be at first," I agreed, glancing at Maizy.

"That's the glorious mystery of life," Maizy said.

"Well, there's no mystery to what I'm doing tonight." Eunice had polished off both doughnuts and was scouting for a third. "I've got a date with an aspirin bottle and a heating pad."

"You ought to try meditation," Maizy told her. "Better than pharmaceuticals. Find your center. Listen to the silence."

I could have used a little more silence out of her.

"Is she for real?" Missy asked me.

"I'm as real as it gets," Maizy said.

"Meditation," Eunice said thoughtfully. "You don't have to talk when you meditate, right?"

I rolled my eyes. "Not unless you meditate in front of the Supreme Court."

The door was closing behind me when I heard Eunice crash to the floor in a dead faint.

* * *

"Sybil Thorpe called me," I told Maizy.

We were at the Lincoln Diner, our favorite of the fifty South Jersey diners along a ten-mile stretch of highway. The Linc was a throwback to simpler if less aesthetic times: red vinyl booths equipped with little jukeboxes, wall-length Formica countertop with swivel stool seating, ginormous bakery case stocked with cakes and cookies on steroids, heavy laminated eight-page menu.

"She was pretty upset," I went on. "She said Abigail's trying to implicate her in Oxnard's death, and she wants me to put a stop to it."

"So the finger pointing has begun," she said. "It was only a matter of time with that much money at stake." She fished an ice cube out of her water glass and popped it in her mouth. "You find that will yet?"

I shook my head. "I'm beginning to think Howard didn't draft the original."

"Maybe not," she said. "Maybe Oxnard used one of those do-it-yourself legal forms websites. If we could check out his computer, I could find out for sure."

We waited until the waitress delivered our dinners. Salmon for Maizy with roasted vegetables. A burger and fries for me. I pretended I didn't notice her nose wrinkling when she saw my plate.

I sampled a fry. Much better than roasted carrots. Better still with a pool of ketchup. I emptied half the bottle onto my plate. "I didn't even see a computer in the mansion," I said.

"Maybe you were distracted by hormones. I hear that can happen in menopause." She slid the Polaroid of Rod Rockstone across the table. "What were you doing with this, anyway?"

"I am *not* menopausal, Maizy." I snatched it up and stuffed it in my bag. "And the question is what were *you* doing with it."

"Research." Maizy ate a carrot. "Brody Amherst has a long way to go. He doesn't even have chest hair."

I didn't want to think about Brody Amherst and his chest hair. "Oxnard must have kept his computer in the office Dusty mentioned," I said.

"Way ahead of you," Maizy said. "My friend Herbie Hairston's cousin Moe works for the custodial company that cleans the offices in that building every night. Moe agreed to let us in around nine o'clock. For fifty bucks, he'll even take a half hour lunch break."

"I don't have fifty bucks," I said. "Will he take a fifteen-minute break for twenty?"

"Don't worry about it," Maizy said. "I've got it covered. I'm loaded. I did Honest Aaron a favor."

My eyes narrowed. "What kind of favor?"

"Nothing like that," Maizy said. "His wife took an earlier flight home to try to catch him with his girlfriend. Lucky for him, I'd just brought back the Bentley, so I covered for him. He gave me a hundred bucks to be Bambi's best friend."

"A hundred bucks?" I repeated. "Does Bambi need another friend?"

"Bambi's got all she needs," Maizy said. "In every respect. Except she's got some windows open upstairs, if you know what I mean."

At the moment I was feeling a little drafty myself.

CHAPTER THIRTY-TWO

––––––

Moe was a surprisingly average looking twenty-something with a lean, muscled build and a narrow ponytail that hung below his shoulder blades. He hustled us across the lobby to the elevators. "Third floor, west corner," he told us. "It's unlocked. Knock yourself out. I myself feel the need for a beverage."

Maizy passed him some bills. "You rock, dude."

Moe nodded without expression. "I know," he said, and disappeared down the hall.

Maizy and I rode the elevator up to the third floor, bypassed a cluster of cubicles, and found the office in the west corner. Pretty standard issue as far as offices went. Heavy furniture, filing cabinet, a couple of abstract paintings on the wall. And a monster 34-inch computer monitor sitting on the desk, with the tower tucked into its own cubicle underneath.

"Sweet," Maizy said, heading for it. "It's already running. That's never a good idea. You never know who could access the system." She pulled on a pair of thin latex gloves and sat down. "This shouldn't take long. He did half the work for me already."

I stayed right where I was. There was nothing I could do but get in her way. "I can't imagine he'd do his own will, with all his money," I said.

"Rich people are like that," Maizy said while she worked. "Cheap. Why don't you see if you can find anything in the filing cabinet. Here." She handed me a pair of gloves.

The filing cabinet had two drawers but needed three. Both were crammed with manila files and mailing envelopes and DVDs. Like in his home office, Oxnard had had everything carefully labeled, making it easy to find the one featuring Dusty Rose.

My lip curled on its own accord. I felt dirty just looking at it. I kind of liked Dusty, and she'd been treated horribly. It took a second to remember she might have gotten her revenge by killing Oxnard. I slipped the DVD into my handbag. I couldn't do anything about what might be online or in anyone else's hands, but I could make sure no one saw that particular copy.

Next I turned my attention to the files. Papers regarding the sale of No Flows and investments Oxnard had made and money he'd lost. A lot of money he'd lost. Either Oxnard had been a serious shopaholic or Herman Kantz wasn't much of a financial adviser.

A smallish manila envelope had been tucked between folders, unlabeled and unsealed, practically begging me to take a peek. It was full of photographs of Sybil and Herman Kantz. Outside the Philly Art Museum, the Academy of Music, on the town, in formal dress and casual. Hand in hand. Sybil smiling up at him like an enraptured teenager. Herman kissing her.

I sat back on my heels. "Maize."

"Huh?"

"Check these out."

I held up the photo of Sybil and Herman in a lip-lock on Penn's Landing with the Delaware River seething in green-brown ripples behind them.

Maizy snatched it from me. "Sybil was doing nicky-nack with the financial adviser?"

It made sense. "Sybil introduced Oxnard to Herman," I said. "I bet they set this all up. Marry Oxnard, get her hands on his money, and bump him off so she and Herman could live happily ever after."

"She could've just waited," Maizy said. "Not like he was going to live much longer."

"We don't know that," I said. "He could have been one of those people you see on the news celebrating their 103rd birthday."

"You mean he wasn't there yet?" Maizy asked.

I rolled my eyes. "Are you finding anything on the computer?"

"Online poker and porn sites. I think this was Oxnard's equivalent of a man-cave."

My eyes fell on a file. "Except." I pulled it from the drawer and flipped it open.

Maizy peeked over my shoulder. "Is that his will?"

I nodded while I scanned it, skipping the boilerplate and heading to the specific bequests. Abby was set to inherit the bulk of his estate. Alston would receive a token amount, which I knew was designed to forestall a potential challenge to the entire will. And Bitsy Dolman was the beneficiary of a cool half a million dollars.

"They really were old friends," Maizy said.

No mention of Sybil. "This had to be the old will," I said. "Before the revisions."

"He did it himself, didn't he?" Maizy said. "There's no lawyer's name on there."

"There's software for that," I said. "But he must have wanted advice about changing it, so he asked Howard to do it."

"Have you been able to find that?" Maizy asked. "Seems like it could be important."

That would be my first job back at the office. Oxnard would never be able to sign a new will, of course, but it might have answers we needed. I folded it up and stuck it in my handbag next to the DVD, ignoring that creepy stealing-from-a-dead-guy sensation.

The elevator *dinged* announcing Moe's return, followed by his whistling approach in our direction. He stopped at the doorway, staring. "You're still here."

"Chill," Maizy told him. "I'm out of money."

We brushed past him, headed for the elevator.

"Come back anytime," he called after us. "I can do fifteen minutes for ten bucks or ten for five."

"We should've waited for the sale," Maizy said.

CHAPTER THIRTY-THREE

———

Maizy showed up at my apartment the next night carrying a pizza box and a bag of something that smelled like wet weeds. When she emptied its contents onto a plate, it looked worse than it smelled. Sort of like coiled earthworms in a mud sauce. "Dinner is served," she said. "Got a fork?"

I slapped one onto the counter. "I'm not eating that."

"Naturally," she said. "I got you some slices."

I carried the box into the living room, where we settled in front of the TV. Ashley sat on the coffee table, watching raptly as Maizy ate. Ashley wasn't a pizza cat. Even though it had sausage and green peppers. No accounting for cat taste.

"So I did some more checking into the bank account thing," Maizy said.

"Whose bank account?" I asked. Couldn't be mine. She'd be wasting her time.

Someone knocked on my door.

"Hold that thought," I said.

Sybil Thorpe launched herself into my apartment the second the door opened, with a lot of arm waving and screeching in a language that may or may not have been English. When she finally stopped for breath, she said "Can you believe it?" and jabbed her hands against her hips. Her fingers were curled into fists. Her stringy arms were taut with Pilatesized muscle. Her jaw muscles were clenched.

I hadn't understood a word she'd said. "You remember Maizy."

Sybil glanced into the living room. Maizy glanced back and kept eating.

"Didn't you hear what I just told you?" she demanded.

"Not really," I admitted.

"There's been a huge withdrawal from your bank account," Maizy said. "To the tune of a couple hundred thou. And you didn't make it."

Sybil's mouth fell open.

I tried to hide my surprise.

"And now you're bouncing checks because you've got eighty dollars left," Maizy added. "You ought to take care of that. That's bad for your credit score."

"Is that right?" I asked. "Someone's stolen your money?"

Sybil's jaw muscles flexed like she was about to tear into some raw meat. "Oh, she's right. And I think I know who did it."

"That dude Herman Kantz," Maizy said.

Duh. I almost did a forehead slap. Of course it was Herman Kantz. Oxnard had probably positioned him to control the money, in effect, handing Herman Kantz a great big checkbook and signatory power.

Wait. Herman Kantz? Kissy-face Herman Kantz?

"What do you know about him?" Sybil growled.

"Not much," Maizy said. "Went to an Ivy and worked for some blue chip companies. Born in Indianapolis. Got an ex-wife named Evelyn and two kiddies and a Yorkie. Mittens."

I supposed that sort of information wasn't too terribly hard to uncover—well, except for the Yorkie part—but it was still pretty impressive.

"Everybody knows that much," Sybil sniffed. "Tell me something interesting."

Maizy shrugged. "He set you up."

Sybil's eyes narrowed into slits. *"What?"*

Maizy held up her cell phone. Simultaneously, Sybil and I reached for it, hesitated, looked at each other, and I drew back, scalded by the fire shooting out of her eyes. She snatched it from Maizy and scrolled down the screen, her lips tightening.

I glanced at Maizy. She was unmoved by Sybil's fury. Maybe because she was out of Sybil's reach. *"What is it?"* I mouthed to her.

Maizy mouthed *"War and Peace"* back to me, at warp speed. I didn't get a word of it.

"Never mind," I mouthed to her.

She shrugged and went back to her plate of worms. "Bet he told you he loved you," she said.

Sybil thrust the cell phone at me. "I'm going to pay him a visit."

Financial Exec Under Investigation. It seemed Herman Kantz, educated at Harvard and the Wharton School of Business, esteemed CFO of several Fortune 500 companies from which he'd been estranged amid unsubstantiated rumors of financial misdeeds I couldn't begin to understand, apparently spelled a potential cinderblock bedroom for Herman if indicted and convicted.

Oh, boy. "Did you know Herman was under investigation?" I asked her.

"Of course not," she snapped. "Why would I get involved with another loser who lied to me?" She frowned a little as if realizing she may have said too much.

Something occurred to me that seemed worth a shot. "Did Herman know anything about Oxnard's will?"

Sybil gave a start. "I'm sure he did. He said he advised Oxie on tax implications. You know Oxie asked Howard to add me as his beneficiary."

Actually, I hadn't known that.

"But Herman told me…" She trailed off.

"That you weren't in the will," I said.

"He's diabolical," Maizy said.

"He manufactured a motive," I said slowly. I met Sybil's eyes. "For you."

Sybil's cheeks were the color of bricks. "He's going to pay for this."

"So you want to confront the dude," Maizy said. "I respect that."

"I don't want to confront him," Sybil snapped. "I want to eviscerate him."

"I respect that, too," Maizy said. "But you might want to play it a little more…" She hesitated, thinking. "…less homicidal."

I held my breath, sure that Sybil would take out her white hot fury on poor defenseless Maizy. But it was my night to be surprised.

"Alright." Sybil crossed her arms, making her biceps bulge. "You're the answer girl. What do *you* think I should do? Let him get away with it?"

Maizy shrugged. "I could talk to him."

"No," I said immediately. "No, you couldn't. She couldn't," I told Sybil.

"Sure I could," Maizy said. "And I'll find out where your money is. For a small finder's fee."

What was this?

Sybil frowned. "I beg your pardon?"

"A finder's fee," Maizy repeated. "You didn't expect to use my expertise for free, did you?"

I thought *expertise* might be stretching it, but I had to hand it to her. Sybil looked like she'd been run over by a cement mixer, and it had parked on top of her.

"Well, I…" She shot me a murderous scowl. "How small?"

"Ten percent," Maizy said.

"*Ten* percent? But that's…" She paused to calculate. "Twenty thousand dollars!"

Twenty thousand dollars? That meant—

"Sounds about right," Maizy said amiably.

But that meant—

"Maize," I said quietly.

"You've got a deal." Sybil stuck out her hand to shake on it. "If the money's back in my account by the end of the week."

Twenty thousand dollars was ten percent of—

"Maizy," I said, less quietly. "May I speak to you?" That kind of money wasn't stolen easily, and it wasn't going to be surrendered easily. There might be more trouble than she could deal with and more than Sybil would expect. There might be violence.

And then there was Herman Kantz's reaction to consider.

"Deal," Maizy agreed. "If he hasn't spent it already. If it was me, I'd have bought a tropical island. Probably be pretty cool, eating coconuts and sleeping on the beach, huh?"

Herman Kantz wasn't sleeping on any beaches, and if he was eating coconuts, they were being hand-fed to him by twelve golden nymphets to the accompaniment of harp music.

"Maizy!" I said with urgency. "You're not going anywhere until I talk to you."

"Oh, stop nagging her," Sybil said. She held out her hand to Maizy with a terrifying smile. "Shall we?"

"I can't let you do this," I said. "Curt would kill me. Cam would kill me."

"Chill," Maizy said. "We won't be in any mortal danger here."

I relaxed only slightly. "How can you be sure?"

"Because *Herman's* going to be the one in mortal danger," Sybil said.

"I'll be back before midnight," Maizy said. "We'll watch *Tattletales*."

"I'm going with you," I said. "I can't let you do this yourself. Just give me a second." I flipped the pizza box closed and hurried to the bathroom to run a comb through my hair and dental floss through my teeth, because one should always be well-groomed when attending an evisceration.

I pulled open the door. "Okay, now I'm—"

The apartment was empty.

CHAPTER THIRTY-FOUR

———

I hauled out my ancient laptop, blew the dust off of it, and powered it on. A Google search for Herman Kantz led me to lots of information about his business ties and former positions with various companies, none of which held any immediate interest to me. There was no personal info, not even the mention of a town of residence. Frustrated, I grabbed the phone to call Information. Nothing. Herman was unlisted in all the ways that mattered at the moment.

I sat slumped at my kitchen table, working up a whole scenario in which Herman Kantz had robbed the Thorpes, seducing Sybil along the way before being discovered by Oxnard or some sharp-eyed executive in the company and reported to the authorities, then found his opportunity to retaliate on Oxnard's wedding night by shoving him in the pool. Maizy liked to say it was always about the money. It looked like she was right.

I planned to tell her so, right before I killed her for running out on me.

Much as I wanted to, I didn't dare tell Curt what had happened. He'd go all alpha male and call his brother, and the entire police force would swarm the area in search of Maizy.

Maybe that wasn't such a bad idea. Except I didn't want to get Maizy in that kind of trouble.

As the time folded in toward midnight and my nerves wound themselves tighter and tighter, I wondered if I should get in the Escort and just drive to the nearest upper class neighborhood. But to do what? Search for the name Kantz on the mailbox? I didn't even know if Herman lived in New Jersey. For all I knew, he was from the Main Line like the Thorpes. Plus, even if I did know where he lived, by the time I got there, Maizy might not be there anymore.

After a lifetime of silence and anxiety, broken only by moments of sheer panic, I heard footsteps on the metal stairs outside. They were back. They had a lot of nerve coming back— I glanced at my watchless wrist—at whatever time it was.

"Okay," I said, rushing to the door, "just so you know, I don't appreciate—"

I'd never seen Sybil like it before. Smiling. It was unnerving.

"Do you two know what time it is?" I demanded.

"I know it's not midnight," Maizy said.

Wrong answer. I could feel my nostrils flaring, and my hands went to my hips of their own accord. In fists. "Where have you been?"

"We went to Herman Kantz's house," she said. "Don't you remember? You didn't take your gingko biloba today, did you?"

Sybil watched her the way a six-year-old watches a kaleidoscope, with utter fascination. Maizy had that effect on people.

I took a deep breath, trying not to let my aggravation show. "What happened with Herman Kantz?"

"Oh, him." She shrugged. "We worked it out. It was epic."

Hopefully without bloodshed. I made a *Get on with it* motion with my hand.

She cocked her head, assessing me. "You seem a little tense. Probably low blood sugar."

Sybil's mouth moved like it wanted to smile again. Two smiles in one night, *that* would have been epic.

"Turns out," Sybil said, "that Herman has an aversion to living in a jail cell. He's decided to return the money. With interest." She glanced at Maizy. "That was a nice touch."

Maizy shrugged modestly. "Of course," she said, "he could still go to jail for killing Oxnard."

"That's his problem," Sybil said.

I grabbed the remote and snapped off the television. "Fine. Well, it's time for you both to go home."

"I kinda thought I'd stay with you tonight," Maizy said. "Seeing as how it'd be dangerous for me to walk home at midnight."

"The Thorpes are living in *my* new home," Sybil said. "And cut her a break. She did a good deed tonight."

"For you," I snapped. "She did the good deed for you. And I'm glad you'll get your money back, because now you can afford to go to a hotel."

"Hotels are cool," Maizy said. "They bring food to your room, and you get lots of TV channels, and someone else makes your bed."

Sybil studied me at length while I fought my innate urge to fidget. I would *not* let her know how uncomfortable she made me. I forced myself not to blink while I stared back at her, trying to project ninja coolness.

Very slowly, she reached into her duffel-sized handbag. "Maybe this will change your mind." She tossed a fat envelope in my direction. I caught it neatly and managed to keep my hands from shaking as I tore it open to find a plump stack of hundred dollar bills inside.

I met her eyes. "What's this?"

"Your friend here insisted on it," she said.

Maizy grinned at me. "It's five grand."

"I..." I didn't know what to say. Visions of paid bills danced in my head. "Thank you," I said finally.

"Don't thank me," Sybil snapped. "I didn't want to do it. It's not like you've done anything to earn it."

"Hey," Maizy said, her tone mild, but something behind the single word drew Sybil up short. "Be nice to her." She glanced at me. "Herman Kantz made a down payment."

"And you're giving it to me," I said with wonder.

Sybil snorted. "Be serious. I've got bills to pay. Lizette Larue is making a pest of herself."

Guess Lizette wasn't satisfied with the old *Check is in the mail* gambit. Now that I knew what Sybil owed her, I couldn't blame her.

"Which reminds me, I really have to change my cell number. Oh, and something else." Sybil dug in her bag again.

"We brought you this." She held out something wrapped in crumpled tin foil.

I approached cautiously, as if it might explode. "What is it?"

"Dessert," Maizy said. "We brought you dessert."

I unwrapped the foil. It was a piece of apple pie.

"You'll want to heat that up," Sybil said. "And put ice cream on it."

I shook my head. "No need." My anxiety had burned off, and I was famished. I studied Sybil while I chewed. "I didn't think you ate desserts."

She shrugged. "I'm learning to be flexible."

If she could be flexible, I guess I could, too. After all, it was getting kind of late to put them out on the street. The envelope full of money left me feeling much friendlier toward Sybil. Suddenly it was hard to see her shoving Oxnard into the pool. Maybe I just didn't want to see it. It occurred to me that maybe Oxnard hadn't been pushed at all. Maybe he'd slipped or tripped and fallen into the pool all on his own, knocking himself out and drowning. A tragic accident, but not murder. I decided I'd go with that to get through the night. And if I was wrong about Sybil, I could rely on Maizy's force field to run interference. So everything was under control.

I should've known better.

CHAPTER THIRTY-FIVE

———

Sybil, Maizy, and I brainstormed for most of the night. I couldn't say it had been useful, but it had been more fun than I'd expected, mostly due to Maizy.

When I got to work the next morning, Mora Dollarz waited in the reception area, sitting ramrod straight, a Coach bag clutched tightly on her lap, her hair caught up into some kind of severe twist and a slash of red lipstick the only color on her face.

I greeted her with an offer of coffee that she waved off. "I'm here to see Mr. Dennis," she said.

"I don't think he's in yet," I told her. "Maybe you'd be more comfortable waiting in the conference room?"

She glowered at me. "Is Mr. Dennis generally late for client appointments? I have another engagement at ten."

Probably had to make a home visit for Smiles for Seniors.

I assured her that he wasn't. A moment later, Eunice came in, swinging a leather portfolio and humming under her breath. She was resplendent in a shapeless sack of a dress and Earth shoes with a peek of white anklet.

She stopped when she saw Mora Dollarz and went a little pale. Before she hit the floor, I hurried over to take her arm. "Breathe," I whispered.

Eunice breathed. "Is that a…is she here for me?"

"She's here for Howard," I said.

"Oh. Oh, good." She let out a long, shaky breath and patted the portfolio. "I have some work to do on that…case we were discussing. I think I know—"

"You!" Mora Dollarz leaped to her feet, pointing a bony arm in Eunice's direction. Once she'd unfolded all those sharp angles, she was shorter than I'd thought, but no less fearsome. "Are you Eunice Kublinski?"

Eunice blinked as if she wasn't sure.

"This is Attorney Kublinski," I said. "But she has a very busy sched—"

Mora was suddenly face-to-chin with Eunice. She was a stealthy little munchkin. "Does the phrase 'improper imposition of curfew' mean anything to you, Attorney Kublinski?"

"I…" Eunice swallowed hard. "It's a legal theory."

"It's nonsense," Mora snapped. "My husband is an attorney, and he's heard of no such thing. How dare you insert yourself into a parent/child relationship? Do you have children, Attorney Kublinski?"

Eunice glanced at me. I shook my head that no, she did not. Her head swiveled back to Mora Dollarz. "I have a Chihuahua," she said.

"A Chihuahua." Mora's nonexistent lips trembled with rage. Probably. "And does this Chihuahua qualify you to solicit an *underage* child as a client to *sue* her *parents* over her *curfew?*"

"Well," Eunice said, "when you put it that way."

"I'll have you disbarred!" Mora shrieked, shaking her finger in Eunice's face. "You are a disgrace to the legal profession! And I'll sue this firm for hiring you in the first place!"

Eunice let out a squeak and crashed to the floor in a dead faint.

Mora Dollarz stabbed her arms across her chest like two sabers, her triumphant gaze shifting to the doorway behind me.

Where Howard had arrived.

* * *

Eunice sat trembling at Paige's desk for the next hour, eating Tums, while Missy and I pretended to be engrossed in typing pleadings. Nobody said anything. About a half hour later, Wally came in, immediately sensed danger, turned on his heel, and went right back out again without a word.

Missy chewed on her lip. "Do you think I should go up there?"

I shook my head.

Missy typed a few words, stopped, and lifted her hands from the keyboard. "I should probably go up there."

"No." Eunice stood up. "I should go."

"Remember the Supremes," I said gently. Missy shot me a questioning look. I waved it off. "That won't end well," I added.

"It probably shouldn't," Eunice said on a sigh. She took a few steps toward the stairs, her feet dragging. "I knew it was only a matter of time."

It was awful. And I didn't know how to stop it. Howard would push her in front of a train if it stopped Mora Dollarz from filing a malpractice suit. And Wally would provide the train schedule.

"Why don't you at least wait a few minutes," Missy suggested. "Until Mrs. Dollarz leaves."

Eunice shook her head. "I should apologize to her. Maybe she won't sue if she knows I'm leaving."

"Leaving!" I sprang to my feet. "You don't have to leave, Eunice. I'm sure Howard will smooth things over. You should have been here when Dougie—"

"I do," Eunice said. "I really do. I should've never come here in the first place. I had no business taking this job."

"Every lawyer has growing pains," Missy told her. "It'll get better."

I wasn't sure about that. But I said, "Sure it will. You should have been here when Wally—"

"It won't get better." Eunice pulled the roll of Tums from her pocket and ate two. "I'd be a lousy lawyer. I don't know what I was thinking. I don't even like it."

"But you can't waste all that education," I said. As far as arguments went, it wasn't very strong, but it was all I could muster. The truth was, Eunice really *wasn't* a good lawyer. She didn't know the law, she didn't know what constituted a viable lawsuit, and she fainted at the sight of black robes.

"I attended the Harvard Academy of Law and Mortuary Sciences," she reminded me. "Online." Another tortured sigh dragged itself out of her. "Ninety-nine dollars for a two-week course."

I glanced at Missy. "You mean for a continuing legal education course," I said. "Right?"

"Wrong." Eunice ate another Tums.

Missy's eyes went wide.

I cleared my throat. "What are you saying, Eunice?"

Eunice tried to shrug, but her shoulders weren't in the right position for it since they were sagging down around her waist. "What I'm saying," she said, "is that I'm not a lawyer."

CHAPTER THIRTY-SIX

———

Howard placated Mora Dollarz out the door a short time later, sighed heavily, scrubbed both hands across his face, pointed Eunice to the conference room, and started all over again, this time from a position of authority. Missy and I tried our best not to listen, but it was hard when phrases like *legal malpractice* and *reality television* and *wring your neck* bled through the walls.

Reality television?

Donna crept downstairs in the thick of it, saw that the conference room was unavailable, and tiptoed back upstairs with an expression of angst, the only one within earshot not interested in knowing what was going on in there.

My fingers were busily skimming across the keyboard while the rest of me was busy not listening, yet nothing but gibberish scrolled across my monitor. I wasn't going to be able to concentrate, not after Eunice's bombshell. Not a lawyer? That explained a lot and nothing at the same time. Missy stabbed at the keyboard with grim determination.

After a while the voices in the conference room quieted, and a little while after that, the door opened and Eunice and Howard appeared, both fairly happy, with no Tums in sight. Howard clapped her on the shoulder and disappeared upstairs.

Eunice dropped into a chair with an exhausted sigh, rubbing her shoulder. "Well, that's that. No more pretend lawyering for me."

I hesitated. "Can I help you pack up your things?"

She brightened. "Oh, I'm not going anywhere. Howard offered me a job as an investigator for the firm. He said I have a real knack for it, that no one really notices me. Isn't that something?"

It was something, alright.

"But you haven't investigated anything," Missy told her.

"Sure I have," Eunice said. "I've investigated a murder. Right, Jamie?"

I ignored Missy's jaw drop. "You told Howard about that?"

"What's she talking about?" Missy asked me. "What are you talking about?" she asked Eunice.

"She doesn't mean murder," I assured her.

Eunice's eyes went wide. "Oh. Right." She laid a finger over her lips and winked at me.

Missy wasn't buying it, but I couldn't help that now.

I sighed. "Eunice, why did you do it?"

"Why does anyone do crazy things?" she said. "To get a reality TV show and become famous. I thought it up while I was watching *Real Housewives*. And you have to admit *Citizen Lawyer* could have been a hit." Her head dropped. "If I could've pulled it off."

Missy and I glanced at each other. Missy mouthed, "*A reality show?*" I shrugged. Not what I would have expected from someone who fainted when more than two people were in the room.

"But now—" Eunice's head snapped up "—maybe I can be *Citizen PI*. Combing the mean streets and alleyways for America's darkest secrets."

"Or going on coffee runs for Howard," I said.

"Either way." She smiled at me, and for once it was a smile filled with genuine happiness. And I was happy for her. Turned out I liked Eunice, and I was glad she was going to be sticking around.

Especially if she could help me find Oxnard's killer on Howard's payroll.

CHAPTER THIRTY-SEVEN

———

It was late afternoon by the time I remembered I'd wanted to call Lizette Larue and the florist about their bills. I waited until Missy had gone upstairs to talk to Howard before I dug out the bills. I dialed Lizette's number first.

"Executive Planning," a pleasant female voice cooed in my ear. A pleasant familiar female voice. Laced with just a hint of alcohol-induced blurriness. I stiffened. "Bitsy Dolman?"

A moment of silence, then, "Who's calling, please?"

I told her. "I was calling for Lizette Larue. About her invoice."

The pleasantness evaporated into a sharp edge that was equally familiar. "Oh, yes. More of Sybil Thorpe's dirty work."

I looked at the bill again. Lizette's contact information was different from Bitsy's, which meant nothing in the age of technology. Still, it was curious. "May I speak with her, please?"

"Lizette isn't available at the moment," Bitsy told me with just the right hint of snit for a company called Executive Planning. "I'll tell her you called."

"Why are you answering her phone?" I asked. "Doesn't Executive Planning have an office staff of its own?"

Bitsy hesitated. "It's an exclusive operation." Read *small*. "I agreed to stand in as her answering service from time to time. Why does that surprise you? I told you I know the best people."

That did make a strange sort of sense, since Bitsy claimed to have recommended Lizette for Sybil's wedding. And clearly she could use the extra money. And get discounted wedding planning services, if she should ever bag Herman Kantz.

"Since I have you," I said, "I wanted to ask you about Fire and Ice. I noticed that it was in Chicago, and I can't see how—"

I heard a click and the line went dead.

Bitsy Dolman had hung up on me.

I dropped the receiver into its cradle, my thoughts churning and my temper flaring. While you'd think I'd have gotten used to it, I didn't like being dismissed. If I was at Executive Planning right now, I'd bean Bitsy with her own vodka bottle. She'd lied to me outright, and now she didn't even have the guts to fess up or the smarts to tell a better lie to cover up her first one.

Which smelled like panic to me. And panic meant guilt. And guilt meant that after a lot of clever bumbling, I may have finally had my woman. Bitsy Dolman, with all her catty judgments and *best people* nonsense, had killed Oxnard, covered it up with a transparent alibi, and didn't know what to do now that she'd been discovered. She was probably packing her Louis Vuitton bag right now to get on the next plane to some country with no extradition treaty.

Not if I could help it.

I glanced at the clock. I could be at the Executive Planning office in ten minutes. But I wasn't going unarmed. I was going to need proof. I raced upstairs to Wally's empty office, grabbed his micro voice recorder, snatched up my handbag, and headed for my car.

"Jamie!" Eunice hustled across the parking lot behind me, breathing hard. "What's wrong?"

I'd forgotten about Eunice. I'd assumed she was off investigating something. "I have to go see someone about a concussion," I said.

"You're not going to do anything foolish, are you?" She leaned on my roof. "I can't let you do anything foolish. You've been too good a friend to me."

"I'm not doing anything foolish," I told her. "I'm doing what I agreed to do."

"Can I do it with you?"

I shook my head. "It won't take long. I just want to put someone in her place." Namely, jail.

"Is it Abigail?"

"No."

"Alston?"

"No."

"That Sybil woman?"

For Pete's sake. I squinted up at her. "Get in, Eunice."

She hurried around the back of the car and tucked herself into the passenger seat, beaming.

"I started to tell you earlier," she said. "I found Howard's notes on the revisions to Oxnard's will. I accidentally stuck them in another file."

"I told you to be careful with that," I said.

"I learned my lesson," she told me. "Don't you want to know what the notes say?"

Of course I did. I'd dreamed about finding those notes, since there was no way I could have asked Howard about them. Howard and I didn't have that kind of relationship. Civil.

"Oxnard was splitting everything evenly between Sybil and Abby," Eunice said.

I frowned. "Anything about Bitsy Dolman?"

"Only that he wanted her removed," she said.

"You sure about that?" I asked. So that childhood friendship had reached its limit. Or Sybil—or Herman—had convinced Oxnard to disinherit Bitsy. It seemed unusual to me that she'd have been a beneficiary in the first place, but then I wasn't a gazillionaire with friends dating back to my diaper days.

"I did a good job, right?" Eunice asked. "Finding the notes?"

I nodded. "Make sure they get back to Oxnard's file."

"Do you think it means anything?"

"I sure do," I said. "It means motive." Bitsy was odd man out when it came to Oxnard's bags of money, probably after years of counting on a hefty payoff for putting up with him. To have the rug yanked out from under like that would have made her furious. Had it made her homicidal?

"We make a good team, don't we?" Eunice said. "Except Maizy isn't here. We need Maizy."

"Not this time," I told her and peeled out of the parking lot.

CHAPTER THIRTY-EIGHT

———

The Hermitage Building was easy to find, since it featured dark glass cladding that leant it a Darth Vaderish appearance. Executive Planning was on the fifth floor, offering stunning views of a parking lot to the north and a murky man-made lake to the west. Fat, white ducks bobbed along the surface of the lake.

Bitsy Dolman slouched behind the front desk, dressed more smartly than usual in white slacks and a turquoise blouse. She was also wearing mud-splattered Nikes. If you couldn't see her feet, she fit the part of a successful businesswoman and was believable for the role of upscale receptionist.

There wasn't a suitcase in sight, but Bitsy wasn't any too happy to see me, and less happy to see Eunice. "What are you doing here?"

"You hung up on me," I said. And that was the least of her offenses.

She shrugged. "I had nothing more to say."

"Well, *we* have something to say," Eunice piped up.

Bitsy pointed with her chin. "Who's this?"

Eunice stepped forward, confident now that she wasn't facing Supreme Court Justices or disgruntled clients. "Eunice Kublinski, PI." She glanced over her shoulder at me with a grin.

"That works," I told her.

"It does, doesn't it," she agreed.

Bitsy snorted. "Well, I'm not interested in what either one of you has to say. How about that."

"You will be," I said, moving next to Eunice while reaching into my jacket pocket for the micro recorder. It wasn't there. "We know what you did."

"What I did." Bitsy didn't blink. "What did I do?"

Eunice stabbed the air with her finger. 'You killed Oxnard Thorpe and we can prove it!"

I shoved a hand into my other pocket. Nothing. "Not yet," I whispered.

"I most certainly did not," Bitsy said calmly. "I loved that man."

"Ah-ha!" Eunice nearly shouted. "You loved that man too much, and we can prove it!"

I patted the pockets of my slacks. Empty. "Slow down," I whispered. "I can't find—"

"Loved him too much?" Bitsy repeated. "What does that even mean?"

"You couldn't stand to see him with another woman," Eunice forged on, undaunted by my growing panic and Bitsy's scary calmness. "When he married Sybil, he told you he was cutting you out of his will, and it put you over the edge. If you couldn't have him—"

"I suppose you have proof of this," Bitsy said to me.

There was only one place left to look.

"Can I smoke in here?" I asked. Without waiting for an answer, I plunged my hand inside my purse, flapping it around in there.

"I didn't know you smoked," Eunice told me.

"Oh, yeah." ChapStick. Wallet. Tissues. Why did I have so many tissues? "Two packs a day. Can't go five minutes without—" There! I wrapped my fingers around it and fumbled for the *On* button. "Oh, we have proof," I said, at the same time Wally said, "Please be advised that this office—"

Eunice immediately began coughing spastically. I jabbed at the *Off* button

"—represents Don Wilfork with regard to—"

Why did they make those damn buttons so tiny?

"Oh, excuse me," Eunice said, patting her chest.

"—his claim for size discrimination in relation to—"

Eunice's eyes widened and met mine.

I stared back at her. "Seriously?" I said. I punched every button I could feel until Wally shut up. "You should get a raise," I told her.

"Well, if it isn't the Two Stooges," a voice said behind us. I knew that voice. It was capable of freezing grown women in a single breath, and it did just that. We didn't move when Lizette Larue sauntered past us in ridiculously high heels and an incredibly tight skirt, holding a terrifying—

I blinked. "Is that a cake server?"

Lizette shrugged. "You use what you've got."

"And what you've got," Bitsy added with a slow phony smile, "is trouble. As usual, you have it wrong."

I was starting to see that. I could also see that Lizette was wearing the green cashmere sweater I'd seen twice before. Once on her, at Sybil's wedding, and once at Bitsy's house. On Bitsy.

Eunice was getting the pasty face that meant she wasn't going to stay vertical much longer.

"I like your sweater," I said, grasping to make sense of it. And I think I finally had it, or at least part of it. "Looks better without the stains," I added pointedly. "You'd think a personal shopper would be a smarter dresser. Of course, if only Herman Kantz and Sybil hadn't beaten you to Oxnard's money, you could've bought all the clothes you wanted. For you and your daughter."

Bitsy's tipped her head to the side, assessing. "So you're not as useless as you seem."

That didn't really call for an answer, so I slid a glance toward Eunice. She was swaying slightly, but still upright.

"Ah-ha!" Eunice cried out, but her heart wasn't in it this time. "So you wanted the money!"

Lizette waggled the cake server in Eunice's direction. "Is she for real?" She stopped waggling and pointed the cake server straight at Eunice. I took a step sideways so I could catch her if she went down. "*Everyone* wanted the money," Lizette hissed. "I'm just the one who deserved it."

"*You!*" I said, at the same time Eunice said, "You?"

I said "*Her?*"

"Don't look so shocked," Bitsy said flatly. "She's right. She always deserved it. She's Oxnard's daughter. Oxnard seduced me when I was only twenty-two, and then he walked away when I told him I was pregnant. He wanted nothing more to do with me. He just moved on to the next *actress*. Don't even get me started on *them*."

"You could have taken him to court," I said, just as flatly.

"Court." She blew out some air. "Sure, I tried that. He played golf with the judge every Wednesday. He was ordered to pay the royal sum of $75 a month in child support. *After* insisting on a DNA test. I mean, can't you see she's the spitting image of Oxnard?"

Sure enough, there were Oxnard's beady little eyes. Why hadn't I seen that before?

"He *owed* his daughter," Bitsy insisted. "He owed me. And I was damned well going to make sure she got every penny she deserved."

"But you stayed friendly," I said. "He invited you to his wedding. How could he not—"

"Friendly." She snorted. "He strung me along, said he'd take care of both of us if I just kept quiet about paternity. So I did. And he kept his agreement. For a while. Told me I'd be in his will to make up for everything. Paid my bills."

"Including your ritzy business address," I said.

"Including that." She smirked. "And then one day he tells me I'm out. The *mother* of his *child* isn't entitled to a dime of his estate. So where did it get me to be the good little soldier?"

"It got you inside his house," Lizette said with an evil little cackle.

"And you got *her* into the hidden hallway," I said to Bitsy. "And then you made sure the food fight escalated so that no one was paying attention when you slipped into the hidden hallway."

She shrugged. "It was just a bonus that they left. It made Liz's job so much easier. She *is* his rightful heir."

"The joke's on you," Eunice said, her voice thin but not shaky. "You killed him for nothing. His will never got changed."

"You're lying," Bitsy said.

"No, she isn't," I said. "Eunice here never prepared it."

"See," Eunice added, "I'm not a lawyer."

"So you could have inherited millions," I said. "Only now you'll go to jail for murdering the golden goose." I didn't know if that was true, but it sounded good. Unfortunately, it didn't seem to sound good to them, since Lizette charged toward me with the cake server raised like a knife. "I've heard enough out of you," she hissed.

That's when Maizy burst through the door behind me, blue hair flying. I was never so happy to see her, or the cake box she seemed to be carrying.

Cake box?

She hustled past me, flipping the lid open as she went, and intercepted Lizette just as she was about to slash me with the cake server, shoving the box in the way so that instead of plunging into me, it plunged directly into—

—a chocolate cake?

She grinned at me. "I know you like chocolate."

"I love chocolate," I agreed. "But I may never eat it again."

Eunice hooked a finger over the cake box, peered inside at the carnage, and her eyes rolled back in her head before she crashed to the floor.

CHAPTER THIRTY-NINE

———

I was wrong. I did eat chocolate again, back at my apartment a little while later, and I ate it pretty efficiently, right down to the crumbs. It was easier than I expected, considering how close I'd been to becoming a shish kabob, but the fat envelope of money from Sybil helped soothe my nerves. Hard to believe the day could end this way, when just three hours ago, I'd been staring death by cake server in the face. Now, with the help of Maizy's earwitness testimony, Bitsy and Lizette had both been charged with murder and accomplice to murder, respectively. And Herman Kantz had dodged an SEC complaint for the moment. Dusty Rose was free to become a makeup artist and to continue the hunt for a more effective rash ointment.

And Abigail and Alston…

Maizy and I were on the floor with Ashley. Sybil was sitting in my recliner, sipping white wine. Eunice was in recovery mode on my sofa with a little smile on her face.

"So," Sybil said, "Bitsy and Oxie had a daughter. No wonder Oxie pushed Lizette Larue's services so hard."

"To be fair," I pointed out, "Oxnard did deny his own daughter for years. It couldn't have been easy for Bitsy."

"Boo-hoo," Sybil said. She looked at Maizy. "And here you come to the rescue."

She shrugged. "It's what I do. Spread the word."

I turned to her. "How did that happen, exactly?"

"My yoga teacher's in the building," Maizy said. "I was in upward facing dog when I saw you two pull into the parking lot."

"And you just happened to have a chocolate cake on you?" Sybil asked. She seemed amused.

"Well, I couldn't very well leave it in the car," Maizy said. "It gets hot in there. I wanted to bring it over later, when I came over to watch *Big Bang Theory*. Jamie's got a thing for chocolate. Well, and Uncle Curt, but especially chocolate."

I might've put those in a different order.

"So I watched where you got off the elevator, and me and the cake came up for a visit. I visited almost every office on the floor." She frowned. "Those people in 5-F are harsh."

"It turns out," Sybil said, "that Herman Kantz gave her the money just like he promised." She gave Maizy a beatific smile and patted her Chanel bag, which must have contained her checkbook, fattened up again.

"I'm loaded," Maizy said.

"And she's a humanitarian," Sybil added. "She convinced me it was only right to give a larger portion of Oxie's estate to his brother and sister. So I did."

I didn't hide my skepticism. "Define a portion."

"A cool two mil," Maizy said.

"I'm still not sure about that," Sybil said with a hint of ice.

Maizy gave her a look.

"Then again, fair is fair," Sybil said.

Maizy smiled at me. "See? I told you we rock as detectives."

"One of us definitely does," I agreed.

"*In loco parentis*!" Eunice yelled.

ABOUT THE AUTHOR

From her first discovery of Nancy Drew, *USA Today* bestselling author Kelly Rey has had a lifelong love for mystery and tales of things that go bump in the night, especially those with a twist of humor. Through many years of working in the court reporting and closed captioning fields, writing has remained a constant. If she's not in front of a keyboard, she can be found reading, working out, or avoiding housework. She's a member of Sisters in Crime and lives in the Northeast with her husband and a menagerie of very spoiled pets.

To learn more about Author, visit her online at
www.kellyreyauthor.com

Enjoyed this book? Check out these other fun reads available in print now from Gemma Halliday Publishing:

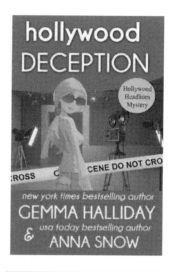

www.GemmaHallidayPublishing.com

Made in the USA
Columbia, SC
02 May 2024

35200096R00126